KT-461-343

KILL THE TOFF

KILL THE TOFF

John Creasey

CHIVERS
THORNDIKE

This Large Print book is published by BBC Audiobooks Ltd, Bath, England and by Thorndike Press®, Waterville, Maine, USA.

Published in 2006 in the U.K. by arrangement with Tethered Camel Ltd.

Published in 2006 in the U.S. by arrangement with Tethered Camel Ltd.

U.K. Hardcover ISBN 1–4056–3536–3 (Chivers Large Print)
U.K. Softcover   ISBN 1–4056–3537–1 (Camden Large Print)
U.S. Softcover   ISBN 0–7862–8148–0 (British Favorites)

Copyright © John Creasey 1950, John Creasey Ltd. 2005.

All rights reserved.

The text of this Large Print edition is unabridged.
Other aspects of the book may vary from the original edition.

Set in 16 pt. New Times Roman.

Printed in Great Britain on acid-free paper.

British Library Cataloguing in Publication Data available

Library of Congress Cataloging-in-Publication Data

Creasey, John.
    Kill the Toff / by John Creasey.
       p.   cm.
    "Thorndike Press large print British favorites."—T.p. verso.
    ISBN 0–7862–8148–0 (lg. print : sc : alk. paper)
    1. Toff (Fictitious character)—Fiction. 2. Private investigators—
    England—Fiction. 3. Large type books. I. Title.
PR6005.R517K55 2005
823'.912—dc22   2005027016

Foreword

RICHARD CREASEY

The Toff—or the Honourable Richard Rollison—was 'born' in the twopenny weekly *Thriller* in 1933 but it was not until 1938 that my father, John Creasey, first published books about him. At once the Toff took on characteristics all his own and became a kind of '*Saint* with his feet on the ground.' My father consciously used the Toff to show how well the Mayfair man-about-town could get on with the rough diamonds of the East End.

What gives the Toff his ever-fresh, ever-appealing quality is that he likes people and continues to live a life of glamour and romance while constantly showing (by implication alone) that all men are brothers under the skin.

I am delighted that the Toff is available again to enchant a whole new audience. And proud that my parents named me Richard after such an amazing role-model.

Richard Creasey is Chairman of The Television Trust for the Environment *and, for the last 20 years, has been an executive producer for both BBC and ITV.*

It was John Creasey who introduced him to

the world of travel and adventure. Richard and his brother were driven round the world for 465 days in the back of their parents' car when they were five and six years old. In 1992 Richard led 'The Overland Challenge' driving from London to New York via the Bering Strait.

CHAPTER ONE

'The Best Way To Disappear . . .'

Mellor flinched as if the pale blue paper were red-hot, dropped it and backed away as it fluttered to the thread-bare carpet. The pale blue envelope, torn where he had ripped it open, quivered in his left hand. Except for this trembling he stood still, watching until the letter settled. Even then he could read the black, block capitals.

THE BEST WAY TO DISAPPEAR IS TO DIE

Suddenly he screwed up the envelope and flung it across the tiny room. It hit the wall, dropped on to the unmade bed and rolled down the heap made by his red-and-white-striped pyjamas. It quivered on the edge, then fell to the floor.

'I can't stand it, I just can't stand it any longer.'

He read the message again; then stared at the gas fire where the broken white mantles looked like bleached bones.

He spoke again, as if someone had been arguing with him: 'No, I just can't stand it any longer.'

His trembling stopped, he picked up the

1

letter and looked down at it. Something like calm settled on his haggard face and his red-rimmed, bloodshot eyes.

He said: 'I'd better get it over.'

He laughed; and he hadn't laughed for days. Days? He hadn't laughed for weeks—not since dread had first cast its shadow over him, not from the moment when he had decided that he must disappear.

It had seemed so easy and proved so great an ordeal; and he had failed because 'they' knew he was here. He didn't know who 'they' were: not the police who would come and arrest him, giving no warning, if they knew where he was. He didn't know who had plotted his death and driven him to desperation. 'They' was a vague, nebulous word, describing the unknown. In less than a month they had turned him from a normal, cheerful, vigorous young man into a physical and nervous wreck.

He had fought them by himself because there was no one to help him; but he couldn't fight any longer. Hunger had added the final touch of fear and that stark message gave him the simple answer to his problems.

He went to the window and looked out on to drab backyards of poor little houses, shrugged, turned and sat in a wicker armchair. It creaked and sagged. He leaned back with his eyes closed. A piece of broken wicker scratched his neck and he shifted his position.

He sat still for ten minutes. Downstairs a door banged; outside a dog began to bark. Before that letter had come the noises would have made him jump; now he was numb.

He opened his eyes and stared at the door; he had been sitting here when the envelope had been thrust beneath it.

He had heard no sound until a faint rustling had made him look up. Every nerve in his body had become taut as he'd seen first the corner, then the whole envelope. Whoever had brought it had flipped it smartly when half of it was inside, making it hit sharply against the edge of the carpet.

The messenger had crept away as silently as he had come.

Clutched by the now-familiar choking fear, Mellor had gone to the door and unlocked it stealthily, opened it and peered out on to an empty landing and an empty staircase. Then he had returned, picked up the letter and ripped it open . . .

Now he wasn't so frightened because he knew what to do. He had been planning every detail while sitting and thinking. The door and the window would have to be blocked somehow, to prevent air coming in and gas escaping, thus warning others in the house before he was dead. The ideal thing would be cotton-wool or gummed paper but he had neither. A sheet or his pyjamas, torn into small strips, would serve; but that would be a laborious job and he had little patience left.

He got up and went to the bed, pulled the grubby pillowcase off and punched the hard pillow. It wasn't made of feathers. He took out his penknife, slit the ticking and pulled out some dirty-looking grey flock.

That would do!

He grabbed a handful of flock—and nicked his finger with the knife. He stood rigid, looking at the tiny red globule that oozed up.

Perhaps the best way to kill himself would be to cut the main artery.

He began to tremble again.

No, he couldn't stand the blood spurting out. He would have to feel it drain from him and would try desperately to stop it. Gas was the best way. Once he got used to the smell it would be easy and peaceful. He'd drop off to sleep, that was all.

Sleep itself would be worth while. He had slept so little of late, moving furtively from place to place, haunted by his fear as well as hunted by unknown men. Had 'they' known every one of his hiding-places? Until the note had come he had believed that he was fooling them but his brief respite may have been part of their damnable cat-and-mouse game. That didn't greatly matter now that he had made his decision.

The best way to disappear was to die . . .

He began to stuff the dusty flock round the side of the door and lost himself in the task. It wasn't difficult but would take longer than he had hoped; pity he hadn't some cotton-wool or adhesive tape. He almost forgot why he was doing it. The feeling of relief from unbearable tension remained, bringing with it a sense not far from exhilaration.

Now and again the dust made him sneeze.

*   *   *

In the rest of that house and outside, the people of the East End of London went about their daily round. Women hurried along dingy streets to tiny shops, traffic grumbled along the wide, sprawling main roads, smoke rose sluggishly from countless chimneys and added to the gloom of the early Spring day.

*   *   *

Judith Lorne sat over the drawing-board, wishing drearily that her drawings would come right. She had been both wishing and trying for hours. They weren't right and it was useless to take these sketches to an editor who knew exactly what he wanted. Judith also knew that; and usually she could satisfy him without great difficulty but these were just so much waste-paper. Her fingers seemed stiff and the pencil wouldn't run smoothly, because every time she drew a man's face, the man looked like Jim. She couldn't get away from

5

Jim. These were to be illustrations for a story in a woman's magazine—a story with a superfine hero and a double-dyed villain—and she couldn't make a face look heroic or villainous; only like Jim.

The light was dull and that didn't help but if the light were perfect she wouldn't be able to do much better. She'd fought against admitting it but, since Jim had disappeared, something of her had gone. It was chiefly her power of concentration. She didn't think she would get it back until she knew what had happened; even if it proved to be the worst and he was dead.

She dropped her pencil and stood up. Jim's framed photograph, with the back towards her, stood on one side of her desk. She picked it up and he smiled at her. That smile had done something to her from the first time she had seen it. It had gaiety, vitality—*life*. Zest for life had been the common bond between her and Jim from the beginning of their friendship. The friendship had grown swiftly, become much deeper and swept them away till they were wildly in love.

There had been five glorious months of planning and preparation, of learning each other's foibles, deciding when to marry, where to live and how. They'd been so crazy that they had decided how many children to have, what sex and what they should be called. They'd even made up a silly doggerel about them, each last line ending:

. . . with Charles, Peter and Anne!

and they'd sung it to the catchy tune of *Peggy O'Neil*, one or the other of them strumming on the old piano which was out of tune and had two broken wires. On the piano, in its rosewood case, was another picture of Jim— like the picture which the police had taken away.

Jim wasn't a murderer.

No man who could laugh and sing and play the fool, be so earnest and grave one moment and full of gaiety the next, could kill a man in cold blood. Downstairs the front door banged.

It always banged when Jim came but, of late, her heart hadn't jumped on hearing it and she hadn't waited for a few sickening minutes to see whether he had returned. He wouldn't return; she had to make up her mind to that. But—there were still dreams. Or memories which had turned into dreams.

She would seem to hear him running up the stairs and humming *Peggy O'Neil*, waiting until her hand was at the door and then bursting out: '*With Charles, Peter and Anne.*' Then he would grab her by the waist and lift her—a trick-hold he had perfected, for she was no feather-weight. He would carry her over to the window, demanding to know what she'd been doing with her time that day and had she

7

earned enough to keep him in idle luxury for another week?

And there had been the times when he had walked up slowly and soberly and been earnest and solemn, hugging her tightly, and saying: 'Sorry, I'm a bit low to-day. What a mess the world's in! Got me down rather, so I've come for some cheering up.'

After a while they'd think of Charles, Peter and Anne—a panacea for all the moods of gloom.

It was twenty-nine days since she had seen him.

On the first she had been worried and puzzled; on the second, frantic; on the third, horrified. For the police had come and asked a great number of questions about him and taken away a few oddments he'd left in the two-roomed flat, including a copy of the photograph. They hadn't told her why they'd come but they had left a man in the street to watch. Next day his photograph had appeared on the front page of all the newspapers. *James Arden Mellor whom the police wish to interview in connection with the Nelson Street Murder.* Day after day paragraphs had appeared about him and the fact that he'd disappeared. But after a while he stopped being news and the police stopped watching her and following her about.

Her friends and acquaintances, landlady and neighbours, no longer looked at her curiously or sympathetically or maliciously. Life went on much as it had before she had met him. But she had changed—she was older, there were times when she felt careworn and thought she looked haggard. At twenty-five! She was in love with a man she might never see again, whom the world believed to be a murderer, but—

He wasn't a murderer; it was fantastic nonsense and she wouldn't pay heed to the evidence, damning though it was. She—

She caught sight of something at the foot of the door. It hadn't been there a moment before. It looked like a piece of paper and she could see only the corner. It was pale blue in colour and someone was pushing it slowly beneath the door. It was an envelope—and suddenly it shot across the polished boards and struck the edge of a large rug. She stared, incredulously; and then suddenly rushed across the room and opened the door.

She heard footsteps.

On the landing she looked over and saw a man running down the last flight of stairs. He had a bald patch in the middle of a dark, oily head of hair. He didn't glance up. He reached the front door, opened it and disappeared; and before she was halfway down the first flight of stairs the door banged again.

When she reached the porch he was out of sight; the house was near a corner which he had rounded. No one else was in the short

9

street with the tall, terraced houses on either side.

A car turned into the street and she would not have taken much notice of it, except for the fact that it was a Rolls-Bentley—Jim's idea of what a car should be. He had planned to buy one, in that wonderful world of make-believe, when he was thirty-seven—eleven years hence. It would be green and they would call it the Queen. This was green. The man at the wheel was glancing right and left, as if searching for a particular house. She noticed that he was good-looking—the kind of man one might expect to find at the wheel of a Rolls-Bentley. Then she went inside, carrying a picture in her mind of the dark oily hair and the bald spot.

She went back to her flat, closed the door and picked up the letter. It was addressed to her in pencilled handwriting.

She tore the letter open, heart thumping now, because whenever he was in a hurry, Jim wrote in an almost indecipherable scrawl like this. She unfolded the single sheet of pale blue paper and read:

'Sorry I've messed things up, Judy. There's nothing I can do now. I didn't mean to kill him. I just felt I had to let you know.'

CHAPTER TWO

The Visitor

The note was signed with a scrawl which might have been 'Jim', might have been almost any short name. The handwriting was shaky—not Jim's usual swift and confident scribble; but it wasn't that alone which made her sure he had not written it.

She read the message again, then looked up at the photograph which was turned towards her.

'Judy,' she said, in an odd, squeaky voice. 'Judy!' She gave a laugh which sounded as odd as her voice and read the note again. 'Judy!' she cried aloud—then started violently as the flat doorbell rang.

She backed away.

Jim had never called her Judy but always— *always*—Punch. It had started at the moment when they'd been introduced, at a tennis-club dance—she could never remember who had actually introduced them. A casual: 'This is Judy, this is Jim,' and the someone had been swept away in the crowd. Smiling eyes in a smiling face had looked at her and a merry voice had said: 'Care to dance, Punch?'

The doorbell rang again.

She folded the letter, put it back in the

11

envelope and opened the door. She had no idea whom it might be; she felt breathless from the discovery, sensing a significance which she couldn't yet understand—and then a tall man appeared in front of her, smiling, vaguely familiar, hatless, wearing a dark grey suit of faultless cut. His eyes held the look that had so often been in Jim's. She felt, not realising what she felt, that she had much in common with this man; they could get along.

'Miss Lorne?'

'Yes.'

'My name is Rollison. I do hope you can spare me a few minutes.'

She had the letter in her hand and wanted desperately to read it again and think about it and try to understand the significance of that 'Judy'. She didn't know this man; for all she knew he had come to sell her something she didn't want. And yet—

He stepped past her while she hesitated.

'Thank you very much.'

His smile faded and his face became grave as he looked at her. She felt that he was assessing every feature of her face in his calm appraisal. Then he moved, easily and swiftly but without fuss and, before she had started to close the door, he was at the window, looking out. She had a feeling that he had forgotten her—put her out of his mind because he wanted to give his attention to something else. She never got over that feeling with him; she never forgot

12

the way he looked while standing close to the wall. If ever she wanted a model for a gay, gallant adventurer, this was the man. The features were finely chiselled, the preoccupation in his gaze was something quite new to her. His eyebrows were dark and clearly marked, the corner of his mouth that she could see was turned down.

She felt instinctively that it would be a mistake to disturb him. The pause seemed unbearably long, although it could have been only two or three minutes, perhaps not even that. Then he relaxed and turned from the window, taking out his cigarette-case as he approached her again.

'Are the police still watching you?' he asked.

The question shattered the atmosphere of calm which he himself had created and her hand poised motionlessly above the cigarettes in the gold case. He stared into her questioning eyes and this time he was smiling.

'They were, weren't they?' he said.

'Yes.'

'Are they doing so now?'

'I don't think so.' She took a cigarette and he lit it for her. 'Why?'

'I wanted to be sure whether you were being watched or I was being followed. Now I think I know.'

She said: 'Are the police following *you*?'

He looked startled and then laughed.

'No. They don't waste their time.'

It was nonsensical to think that he was like Jim. He was half a head taller, his hair so dark that it looked nearly black. Jim's face was rugged and plain, made attractive by his eyes; this man was handsome; and yet—something about him reminded her vividly of Jim. Her glance strayed to the photograph and he didn't look round but said:

'Is it a good likeness?'

'Yes, it is. But what do you want?' Her voice sharpened. 'I'm busy, Mr—'

'Rollison,' he reminded her. 'Why were you downstairs just now?'

She felt inclined to ask him what business it was of his but didn't. She walked to a chair and sat down, smoothing the skirt of the long, green smock which she always wore when working. She was suddenly conscious of being untidy. Jim always said he preferred her fair, curly hair that way; he thought a conventional set spoiled it. She hadn't made up that day because she hadn't been out of doors; she must look dreadful. Her fingers strayed to her hair.

'Don't bother,' said Rollison and his eyes sparkled, like Jim's when he had first called her 'Punch.' 'Why did you go downstairs? Please tell me.'

She was tempted to say 'For a breath of air' but she didn't; yet she couldn't think how to tell him why without sounding foolish and perhaps giving something of importance away.

14

That letter *was* important. So she said:

'I thought I heard the postman.'

'Expecting a letter from Jim?'

She flared: 'What are you getting at? Who are you? I've every right—'

But her voice trailed off because he was smiling at her, not mockingly or to make her feel foolish but as if he were amused and asking her to share the joke.

'I'm Richard Rollison, and I've heard a lot about you. I wanted to find out what you really looked like, what way you did your hair, whether you cared a hoot about Jim or whether he had almost faded out of your mind—all that kind of thing. You see, I'm interested in Jim Mellor's disappearance. Not in Jim himself—we weren't even acquaintances, I'm not a long-lost friend. It still gets you badly, doesn't it? You can't believe he ever killed a man, yet the evidence has piled up against him. To make it worse, he hasn't written and hasn't telephoned you. That's almost as bad as a confession.'

She said: 'He didn't kill that man!'

'Do you know for sure or is that just wishful thinking?'

'He couldn't have done. Not Jim.'

'Why did you look up and down the street?' asked Rollison.

'That's nothing to do with it!'

Rollison went to the desk and picked up the photograph. She saw him glance at the sketches which were so stiff and wooden but his gaze didn't linger for long on them. He studied the photograph and spoke while he was doing so.

'You know, I've a feeling that your jaunt has something to do with Jim. If you ask me why, I couldn't tell you. But Jim's very much on top of your mind just now—more even than usually. He's always there, ready to pop out at a moment's notice, but this afternoon he's in complete possession. Why?'

He put the photograph down and looked at the letter which lay in her lap.

'Is that from him?' he asked gently.

Then suddenly, for no reason at all, hot tears stung her eyes and she turned her face away hastily. She hadn't talked freely about Jim to anyone for twenty-nine days. She hadn't met a soul who really understood what was in her mind, how Jim was with her so often, ready to smile at her or sing 'Charles, Peter and Anne.' Or, if there were a gloomy headline in a newspaper, how he was likely to frown and become earnest and say that, hell, he didn't know what the world was coming to.

She blinked away the tears, sniffed and faced Rollison.

'I wish I knew why you've come,' she mumbled.

'I want to find Jim.'

'Are you—a policeman?'

'I don't want to find him so that he can be

16

handed over to the law for what they call taking his medicine. I think there's real doubt whether he killed that man and the police don't think there's any doubt at all. I'd like to know the truth but even that isn't so important as finding Jim.'

'But—but *why*, if he's a stranger to you?'

'I've been looking for him for some weeks. Before he disappeared.'

'Why did you want him?'

'I didn't want him,' said Rollison and paused, as if weighing every word. 'His father did. His father is a sick man and by way of being a friend of mine. Let's say a friend, anyhow.' His eyes were very bright and he seemed to be challenging her to reject all this. 'And yet, I do want to find him for myself because I made a shocking mistake over him. I talked too much to his father. Ever paused to think you can never take back any word you've said? Trite but true and worth remembering.'

Until Rollison said 'his father,' Judy had felt more relaxed than she had for twenty-nine days. From then on she had started to tense up again and now her nerves and her muscles were taut and her hands were clenched; she still held the letter.

She said: 'Will you please go, Mr Rollison?'

'Not yet.'

'Then will you tell me the truth.'

'I have.'

'That's another lie. Jim had no father.'

17

'That's an illusion; he didn't know he had a father living.' Rollison smiled faintly. 'There's something wrong about that "a father", isn't there?'

'You mean—' she was baffled.

'His name wasn't—isn't—Mellor. It's the name of the family which finally adopted him. Oh, he was known as Jim Mellor, in the eyes of the law he was Jim Mellor, but his real name is Arden. You know it as his second name. His father came to me some time ago and asked me to find him and to prove his identity and afterwards I talked too freely. When I thought I'd found Jim I told the old man and mentioned what name he was living under. There's quite a story. The family who looked after him for the old man passed him on to these Mellors. After I'd talked, there was a story in the newspapers about the murder and the hunt for Mellor. There was also panic among the old man's friends for, as a result, he had a seizure. He's over it now—or as much over it as he'll ever be. He has an odd notion: that his son isn't a murderer. He's as stubborn and illogical about it as you are, with even less reason, because he hasn't seen his son for twenty-six years. He wants to find him and prove himself right. Old men are like that. So, for different reasons, you and he are after the same thing. As I'm helping him, I don't see why I shouldn't help you.' He smiled again and leaned back against the desk. 'Why

18

did you go downstairs?'

*   *   *

Judy told Rollison, and showed him the letter, and explained about 'Punch and Judy.' It was surprisingly easy to speak freely, to pour out the whole story. He was a good listener, intent on every word; and he let her finish before making any comment. She felt more relaxed than she had for nearly a month; this man's visit was good for her. She wasn't wholly convinced that he'd told her the truth because the story seemed fantastic: but she was glad he was here and that she could talk.

She said: 'I'd just realised that Jim would never have written "Judy" when you rang the bell. There isn't any doubt, he didn't write that letter.'

'It looks like their big mistake; bad men always make at least one! Did you see the man who delivered the letter?'

'I only caught a glimpse of him, I didn't see his face. I was at the top of the stairs, he was in the hall. He didn't look up but—' she broke off.

'Yes?'

'It can't help but he had a bald patch—very dark, oily hair and a small white bald patch right in the middle. He seemed short and dumpy, too, but that may have been because I was looking down on him.'

19

'You have a nice, tidy mind,' said Rollison. 'Short, dumpy, oily hair and a bald patch. It's a small world. Did you notice where I stood when I went to the window just now?'

'Yes.'

'I wanted to make sure I couldn't be seen from the street. Have a look for yourself, will you?'

Judith went towards the window. She moved without any feeling of tension or listlessness, only a quick stir of excitement. She stood close to the wall, very conscious of Rollison's gaze, and peered into the wide street. Some way along, on the other side of the road, a man sat at the wheel of a small open car and read a newspaper. She couldn't see a bald patch but his hair was dark and looked very shiny; as it would if it were heavily oiled or greased. Her excitement quickened, became almost unbearable.

'Same man?' asked Rollison.

'I can't be sure but—'

'I think we'd better make sure. Come away from the window, will you? still taking care that he doesn't see you.' She obeyed; it felt slightly ridiculous to move back towards the corner and then approach the middle of the room from the fireplace. But Rollison's manner removed all qualms and her excitement became so intense that she felt suffocated; as if she couldn't breathe freely because of some impending sensation. 'If Jim

20

didn't kill that man, the murderer wants to frame him. Frame—blame—please yourself. That means an ugly business, Judith, perhaps with more than a little danger. There's nothing ordinary about all this and, if murder's been done once, it might be done again. What worries you most? Danger or having Jim damned and consigned to the gallows?'

'What do you want me to do?' she asked.

Rollison laughed.

'Just stay exactly as you are. Jim would hate to find you changed. I'll be back.'

He moved across the room with the swift ease with which he had moved before and the door closed softly behind him. Judith held her breath. He had braced her, given her new hope, presented her with a picture of a glorious future. It wasn't just what he had said or how he looked; it was as if a keen, invigorating wind had swept through the room, blowing away dark fears and dread and lethargy.

She went back to the window so that she could see outside without being seen.

CHAPTER THREE

The Man With Oily Hair

Rollison let the street door bang behind him and lit a cigarette as he went towards his car. He glanced at the two-seater incuriously, paused and smiled when a puppy came frisking along the road at the end of a long lead attached to a staid and stately woman. Then he got into the driving-seat and pressed the self-starter. The engine purred and the car slid towards the near corner and swung round it.

He didn't glance up at Judith's window.

He turned left and left again and yet a third time so that he was back at the far end of Knoll Road. The man in the two-seater still sat at the wheel reading his newspaper and didn't look round. Rollison slowed down until the Rolls-Bentley was crawling along at ten miles an hour. As he drew nearer he saw the bald patch in the man's head; it was clear and white, quite unmistakable. He put the brakes on gently. The nose of the big car drew level with the nose of the small one, passed it, then stopped.

The two drivers were alongside each other.

'Good afternoon,' said Rollison.

The man put his newspaper aside and

glanced at him uninterestedly. He had a pale square face with high cheekbones, red lips and a flattened nose. The shoulders of his coat were thickly padded, giving him a squat and powerful look.

'What is it?'

'I thought we'd have a chat about Judith Lorne,' said Rollison. 'Charming girl, isn't she?'

The dark eyes, fringed with short dark lashes, narrowed a fraction but the man gave no other indication that he knew Judith Lorne or was surprised by this encounter.

'Who?'

'Judith Lorne—Jim Mellor's Judy. Remember Jim?'

The man turned back to his newspaper.

'I don't know what you're talking about,' he said. 'I'm waiting for a friend.'

He pretended to read the paper but shot a swift sideways glance at Rollison.

'I'm the friend,' said Rollison.

He eased off the brakes, slid his car in front of the two-seater, well aware of the other's gathering tension; but the other made no attempt to start his engine and go into reverse. Rollison jumped out, getting a clear view of the man full-face. The broad, square features weren't typically English; the clothes seemed to be of American cut. He saw the other's right shoulder move, as if the driver had shifted his arm, as he drew up by the nearside

23

door.

'Yes, I'm the friend,' he repeated. 'Shall we go and see Judith together?'

'You're crazy,' the man said. His voice showed no trace of an accent; it was hard, rather deep and, now that his lips were parted they revealed small, white, wide-spaced teeth. 'Clear out.'

Rollison opened the door of the two-seater.

The man now had his right hand in his coat pocket and the newspaper spread over his lap. The expression in his dark eyes was both wary and aggressive.

'Take a walk,' he said. 'Don't try—'

Rollison drove his fist into the powerful biceps and, as the man's muscles went limp, pushed the newspaper aside and grabbed his forearm. He jerked the hand out of the pocket and glimpsed the automatic before it slid down out of sight. He jabbed the man's chin with his shoulder and snatched the gun, all apparently without effort. Then he slipped the weapon into his own pocket and backed away. He pulled the newspaper, rustling it past the driver's face, half-blinding him and adding to his confusion, screwed it up into a ball and tossed it into the back of the car.

'Shall we go and talk to Judith?' he suggested mildly.

He slid his right hand into his pocket and poked the gun against the cloth, near the big shoulders.

24

There was a moment of stillness, of challenge. Then the stocky man relaxed and leaned back in his seat. His eyes were dull and his mouth slack.

He said: 'You've asked for plenty of trouble.'

'I don't want to have to deal out any more yet,' said Rollison. 'Come along.'

He half-expected the man to cut and run for it; but after a pause the other gave way and climbed out of the car. Rollison gripped his arm tightly; he felt the powerful, bulging muscles and knew that it would be no fun if this man turned on him. He kept half a pace behind, still holding the arm, and they crossed the road in step and walked towards Number 23. Outside were two cement-covered posts where a gate had been fixed before scrap iron became a weapon of war. As they reached these Rollison felt the muscles tense, knew that the escape attempt was coming and pulled the man round. At the same time the man back-heeled. Caught on one leg, he stumbled and nearly fell. Rollison stopped him from falling, pulled him upright and bustled him into the porch. The front door was unlocked. Rollison thrust it open and pushed the man in front of him.

He said: 'Don't do that again.'

Keeping his hand in his pocket, he jabbed the gun into the small of the other's back. They went upstairs slowly, footsteps firm on every tread. A door on the first landing opened and a faded-looking woman appeared, carrying a shopping-basket. She stared into the glowering face of Rollison's prisoner and started back.

Rollison beamed at her. 'Good afternoon!'

'G-g-good afternoon, sir.'

There were three floors. At the top, Judith's door faced the head of the stairs and, as they reached the landing, the door opened.

'Lock the door when we get in,' said Rollison.

He gave his prisoner a final shove into the room and followed him. Judith closed and locked the door and slipped the key into a pocket of her smock. She looked at Rollison, not at the prisoner who stood with his back to the desk, his hands bunched and held just in front of him. He was shorter than Judith and very broad. The wide spaced teeth showed as he breathed heavily, his nostrils moved, the dark eyes proved to be deep-set and the thick eyelashes gave him an unnatural look. He was spick-and-span: his shoes were highly polished, he wore a brightly coloured tie and a diamond tie-pin. The long jacket of his suit confirmed Rollison's impression that it was of American cut.

'You're asking for trouble,' he said again, thickly.

'We won't go into that again,' said Rollison. 'Sit down.' The man didn't move. 'I said sit down.' He didn't raise his voice but something

26

in its tone made the other shift to a chair and drop into it. 'Judith, go and take his wallet out of his coat pocket.'

Judith obeyed, as if it were an everyday request; but there was no wallet, only some letters.

'They'll do,' said Rollison. 'Who are they addressed to?'

She looked at each of the four before she said:

'Stanislas Waleski at the Oxford Street Palace Hotel. Two say "Stanislas", the others just "S".'

'Thanks. Put them on the desk, will you? So we've a Pole who talks like an Englishman and wears American clothes. Quite a cosmopolitan, isn't he? Waleski, lean forward —farther than that.'

Waleski's head was thrust forward; he studied his shoes and the bald patch showed in the middle of the dark head.

'Well, is that him?' asked Rollison.

'Yes!'

'Good. Do you like getting hurt, Waleski?'

The man leaned back in his chair, his face darker for the blood had run to his head, and his eyes flaming. He didn't speak but clutched the arms of his chair.

'Because you're going to get hurt if you don't do what you're told,' said Rollison. 'Let me have that letter, Judith.'

She handed it to him and he read aloud, very

slowly:

' "*Sorry I've messed things up, Judy. There's nothing I can do now. I didn't mean to kill him. I just felt I had to let you know that.*" '

As the last few words came out, Rollison lowered the letter and looked straight into Waleski's eyes.

'Who wrote that?'

'How the hell should I know?'

'You delivered it.'

Waleski said: 'That's what you think.'

Then Rollison moved again—a swift lunge, startling Waleski and the girl. His right hand shot out and the fingers spread over Waleski's face. He pushed the square head back against the chair with a bump and struck Waleski on the nose with the flat of his hand. Tears of pain welled up.

Rollison leaned back, as if admiring his handiwork.

'Who wrote it, Waleski?'

Waleski gulped and swallowed hard as he tried to speak, pressed his hand against his nose, drew a finger across his eyes. The squat, powerful body seemed to be bunched up, as if he were preparing to spring from the chair. Rollison took the automatic from his pocket, squinted down the barrel then flicked the safety catch off and pointed the gun towards Waleski's feet.

Waleski said: 'I'll kill you for that.'

He didn't shout, didn't put any emphasis

into the words—just let them come out flatly, as if he meant exactly what he said.

Judith felt her own tension returning; something like fear ran through her.

'Yes, you're fond of killing,' Rollison said and his voice hardened. 'You killed Galloway; Mellor didn't. If that note means what I think it means, it's a prelude to the murder of Mellor.' He took no notice of the way Judith drew in her breath. 'It's the kind of note a man might write before killing himself—a confession note. But he didn't write it; you made one fatal mistake, and—'

'*I* didn't write it!'

'You know who did. Where's Mellor?'

Waleski started, caught off his guard by the sudden switch from one subject to another.

Rollison snapped: 'Where's Mellor? Tell me or I'll smash your face in. You think I hurt you just now but you'll find out what it's like to be really hurt if you don't tell me. *Where's Mellor?*'

He levelled the gun at Waleski's stomach and his face took on an expression of bleak mercilessness which pierced Waleski's already shaken composure, made him sit there with his eyes scared and his lips parted, his hands grasping the arms of the chair.

But he didn't answer.

'Get out of the room, Judith,' said Rollison, without looking at the girl. 'I don't want you to see what happens to the obstinate Mr

Waleski. Shut yourself in the kitchen and stuff your ears with cotton-wool.'

He didn't alter the tone of his voice and didn't look away from Waleski.

Judith hesitated.

'Hurry, please.'

She turned slowly towards the door of the tiny kitchen and paused with her fingers on the handle. She saw the two men staring at each other, sensed the clash of wills and the working fear in Waleski, opened the door sharply and stepped into the room beyond. She heard Rollison say:

'I'll give you one minute.'

The door closed.

She stood close against it, her body stiff, staring at the painted wood as if she could see through it into the next room. There was a breathless hush which did not seem to be disturbed by noises from outside. It lasted for what seemed a long time—and then she heard a thud, a cry, a sudden flurry of movement and another thud. She leaned against the door, unable to move and beginning to tremble.

Then Rollison said again: 'Where's Mellor?'

Waleski muttered something; she didn't hear what it was. But as he finished, Rollison called out: 'Judith!'

She flung the door open and went back into the room.

Waleski still sat in the chair; the blood was

30

streaming from his nose and his lips were a red splodge. Blood had spattered his bright tie and his collar and shirt and he leaned back as if he were physically exhausted.

Rollison was rubbing the knuckles of his right hand. His eyes were glowing; obviously he had learned what he wanted.

Yet she burst out: 'Has he told you where—'

'Yes. Is there a telephone in the house?'

'Downstairs, I—'

'Hurry down and telephone Mayfair 81871— my flat. The man who answers will be Jolly or Higginbottom. Say I want Jolly to come here at once and Higginbottom to meet me at the corner of Asham Street—*Ash*am Street, Wapping—in half an hour. Have you got that?'

She was already fumbling for the door-key and nodded as she went out.

'Tell Jolly I won't be in for tea' said Rollison.

*　　　*　　　*

It was as if a miracle had happened.

He had found out where Jim was; had almost proved that Jim hadn't killed Galloway. He had opened up a new, bright world. Judith felt her nerves jumping as she hurried downstairs, slipped on the bottom step and saved herself by grabbing the banister rail. She had to wait for a moment, to get her breath back. Then she tapped on the

31

door of the downstairs flat. The door was opened by Mrs Tirrell, her landlady.

'May I—'

Mrs Tirrell, a short, fat woman with shiny black braided hair, a pendulous underlip and a hooked nose, raised her hands in alarm and exclaimed:

'What on earth's the matter, Miss Lorne? What—'

'I must use your telephone—quickly, please.'

Judith pushed past into a large room crammed with Victorian furniture and bric-à-brac and photographs in sepia and black-and-white. The old-fashioned candlestick telephone was on a round table near the window.

'Well!' gasped Mrs Tirrell.

But Judith was dialling. Mayfair 81871—her finger was unsteady and cold. *They* knew where Jim was. *Brrr-brrr, brrr-brrr.* Would the man never answer?

'Is anything the *matter*?' Mrs Tirrell's voice was shrill.

'No, it's all right.'

Brrr-brrr, brrr-brrr. Perhaps Rollison's flat was empty. If it were, that would mean serious delay—dangerous delay. It was useless to tell herself there was no hurry; she had to see Jim. Minutes counted—seconds counted. It was as if every moment of twenty-nine days was hanging in the balance, dependent on what happened in the next half-hour. A large brass

32

clock beneath a glass cover stood on a wall-bracket, ticking loudly. *Tick-tock, tick-tock; brrr-brrr, brrr-brrr.* It was five minutes to four.

Would they never answer? Jolly or Higginbottom, it didn't matter which—

The ringing sound stopped and a man spoke rather breathlessly: any other time Judith might have smiled at the gasping tone combined with an obvious effort to be precise.

'This is the—residence of—the Hon. Richard—'

'I'm speaking for Mr Rollison. He told me to ask for Mr Jolly or—'

'This is Jolly, madam.'

'You—' She was conscious of the eager gaze from Mrs Tirrell's protuberant, fishy eyes, of the difficulty of saying exactly what she wanted without telling the woman too much and without being long-winded and so wasting time. 'Will you please come here—to 23, Knoll Road, Chelsea—at once? And will you ask Mr Higginbottom to meet—to meet Mr Rollison at the corner of Asham Street, Wapping, in half an hour?'

The man at the other end had regained his breath.

'I have the message, Miss. Who is speaking, please?'

'Judith Lorne.'

'Did Mr Rollison say anything else, Miss Lorne?'

'No! It doesn't—Oh, yes, he did! He won't

33

be in to tea.'

It sounded ridiculous but a change in Jolly's tone when he answered told her that it wasn't.

'Very good, Miss Lorne. I will be there as soon as I can. Good-bye; Mr Higgin—' she heard him call the other man before ringing off.

She stood with the receiver in her hand and Mrs Tirrell prancing about in front of her, desperately eager to know what all this was about.

'You look so pale, dear. Is everything all right?'

'Oh, yes. Yes. Everything's—*wonderful!*' Judith squeezed her hand as she went towards the door and suddenly realised that she hadn't any money with her; it was a rule of the house that all calls were paid for in advance. 'I'll let you have the tuppence, Mrs Tirrell, thank you—thank you!'

She fled and raced up the stairs. She knew that Mrs Tirrell was standing and watching but she didn't care—nothing mattered but getting to Jim. How long would it take Jolly to reach here? Twenty minutes at the most; as the flat had a Mayfair number, it must be in Mayfair. Wasn't she bright? She giggled from reaction, reached the second landing and caught sight of Mrs Tirrell disappearing into her flat. It wouldn't be long before the woman came up to find out what was happening. Her hooked nose was the most curious and intruding one in Knoll Street. Never mind Mrs Tirrell; Rollison could deal with her—Rollison could deal with anyone.

She slowed down as she went towards the top landing. She mustn't lose her head. She had kept her composure well with Rollison: it mattered whether she impressed him favourably or not; he held her future in his hands. She mustn't forget that. He had talked of danger and he wouldn't talk lightly; so there was danger. The way Waleski had said 'I'll kill you for that,' in the cold, dull voice, came back to her and took the edge off her excitement. What kind of affair was this? Who were the people who could frame—frame or blame?—Jim? Who would send her a lying message, a confession note? And then she remembered Rollison saying that if the note meant what he thought it meant, it was a prelude to murdering Mellor—murdering *Jim*. She felt a wave of nausea as she reached the landing and held tightly on to the top rail of the banisters. The landing was dark and gloomy, for the only light came from downstairs and there was a huge mahogany wardrobe which took up almost the whole of one wall.

She must compose herself.

She moistened her lips and went forward. There was no sound from the room—the men weren't talking. She raised her hand to tap— and then something moved, to her right, and

35

she glanced round.

A man darted from the corner by the wardrobe and, before she could move or cry out, one of his hands spread over her mouth. The other grabbed at her neck and she felt the tight clutch of his fingers—a sudden, suffocating pressure.

CHAPTER FOUR

The House In Asham Street

Waleski sat in the chair, occasionally dabbing at his split lips and his nose with a bright yellow-and-red handkerchief. His eyes were dull and he didn't look at Rollison, who stood by the desk glancing through some of the sketches. Now and again Rollison looked up at the photograph of Jim Mellor and smiled faintly.

Judith had been gone a long time; but Jolly would be in; with luck, Snub Higginbottom would be there too. Jolly would look after Mr Waleski; Snub was the better man to have at Asham Street. It was no use speculating on whether Mellor would be alone or whether friends of Waleski would be with him. It wasn't much use asking Waleski for more information—the man had recovered his nerve and would lie from now on.

He might have lied about Asham Street; but Rollison could usually tell when a man had told the truth. He had forced that information out when Waleski had been suffering from both pain and shock, before he had realised the kind of opposition he was up against. But you couldn't use shock tactics against this type of man twice within a few minutes.

Here was Judith, running up the stairs.

Rollison glanced at the door.

The footsteps stopped and he frowned. Then they came again, much more quietly, towards the door. He moved across the room, keeping an eye on Waleski who might be pretending to be completely cowed so that he could try shock tactics himself. But Waleski wasn't tensed to spring from his chair. Rollison actually touched the handle of the door, then heard a faint sound—the sound a scuffle would make. He stopped, hand still poised. He glanced round and saw Waleski sit up sharply, as if he realised the possible significance of this.

There was no further sound outside.

Rollison dropped his right hand to his pocket and the gun; and then Waleski sprang up. Rollison was on the half-turn. He could have shot the man but this wasn't the moment for shooting. He stepped swiftly to one side as Waleski leapt at him, fists clenched, eyes burning. He anticipated Rollison's move and changed direction; and he came like a battering-ram. Rollison jabbed out a straight left. Waleski slipped it with a neat head movement and crashed a blow into Rollison's chest. Then he kicked.

Rollison banged back against the wall.

The glint in Waleski's dark eyes was murderous. He grabbed at the gun, using both hands. Rollison held on, Waleski forced his hand up, bent his head and sank his teeth into the fleshy part of Rollison's hand. Pain, sharp and excruciating, went through Rollison. It took much of the power out of a left swing which brushed the back of Waleski's head.

Waleski leaned all his weight on Rollison, biting harder, drawing blood. The pain made Rollison's head swim. The room seemed to get a fit of the jitters. He released his hold on the gun and it dropped.

Waleski let him go and grabbed at the gun.

Rollison kicked at it, caught the man's wrist with his foot and head with his knee. Waleski lost his balance and backed away unsteadily— and Rollison, leaning against the wall, slid a small automatic out of his hip pocket.

'This makes a nasty hole, too, Waleski.'

His voice was unsteady and his head still whirled. Waleski's face seemed to go round and round. But Waleski moved farther away, the impetus of his effort lost, fear back again. He was afraid not only of the gun but of the deadliness in Rollison's eyes. Together these petrified the man.

38

The first gun lay on the floor near Rollison. Keeping Waleski covered, he bent down and picked it up, glancing swiftly towards the door. There was no sound from outside but the handle was turning. He looked at Waleski who was still held at bay. Waleski licked his lips and raised his hands a little, as if imploring Rollison not to shoot.

Rollison said softly: 'Go into the kitchen.'

Waleski's tongue shot out again and he took two steps backwards.

'Hurry, or—'

Waleski turned and disappeared into the kitchen. Rollison stepped swiftly after him and turned the key in the lock.

Now the flat door was opening slowly. Rollison moved to the wall alongside it. The door was open perhaps half an inch. This must be a friend of Waleski's—a man as deadly and as dangerous and who was fresh for the fight. The moment for shooting had come. Rollison didn't think of Judith, only of the man outside who must have heard the fight, forced the lock while it was going on and prepared for any violence. Rollison watched for a hand, a finger or a gun; but before anything appeared, a woman screamed.

The scream rasped through Rollison's head.

He heard a growl and a flurry of movement, another scream which was cut short by a thud. By then he was at the door. He didn't pull it open but peered round, gun in hand. He saw a

39

small man, with his back to him, striking out at a woman whose hands were raised and who was toppling backwards down the stairs; all he saw of her was a flurry of a black dress and a coil of dark hair; then she fell and screamed again.

The little man swung round.

Rollison said: 'If she breaks her neck, you'll be hanged.'

He went forward, gun thrust out—and the little man turned and raced down the stairs.

If Rollison fired he might hit the woman who was still falling, her heavy body thudding from stair to stair.

The little man leapt over her to the landing and fled down the next flight. Rollison took two steps after him as the woman came to rest; and then he heard a sound from behind him.

It was Judith, getting slowly to her knees, one hand stretched out as if in supplication. In the gloom she looked deathly pale.

He said: 'It's all right, Judith. Take it easy.'

It was too late to stop the little man but he hurried down the stairs to the woman who lay inert, her legs doubled beneath her and one arm bent at an odd angle. Her black hair and clothes threw her pallor into greater relief. He knelt beside her and felt her pulse.

It was beating.

Judith stood at the top of the stairs.

'Where's that telephone?' called Rollison.

40

'In her flat. The ground floor. Shall I—'

'You'd better come down with me,' said Rollison.

He straightened Mrs Tirrell's legs and made sure that no bones were broken; but he didn't touch her arm which obviously had a fracture. He felt her head and discovered a swelling on the back: she had caught her head on a stair and this had knocked her out.

Judith stood unnaturally still by his side.

'Just knocked out. She'll be all right,' he assured her. He looked at the bleeding teeth-marks in his hand, wrapped a handkerchief round it and then took Judith's arm. They went down the next flight of stairs and into the crowded parlour. 'No one seems to have noticed the din, Judith. Are they used to rough-houses?'

'All the other tenants are out during the day.'

'Who's the woman in black?'

'The landlady.'

'Any husband about?'

'No, she's a widow. She—*Will* she get over it?'

'She hasn't broken her neck and her pulse is good and strong, so I really don't think there's much to worry about.' Rollison glanced at the brass clock and seemed to wince: it said twenty-five minutes past four. 'Jolly should be here any minute. I'm going to leave you with him after I've telephoned the police. They'll send a doctor along and look after the landlady and then they'll ask you a lot of questions. Tell them the truth but don't mention Asham Street. If they try to make it hot for you, leave them to Jolly. Don't lie. If they ask a question you don't want to answer, just keep quiet. I don't think they'll be difficult but there are awkward policemen.'

He smiled and squeezed her arm. Then he dialled Whitehall 1212—and as he held the receiver to his ear a taxi drew up outside.

A middle-aged man, dressed in black and wearing a bowler hat, paid off the driver and turned towards the front door.

'That's Jolly,' said Rollison. 'Let him in, will you?'

Judith went out at once and so did not hear what Rollison said to Scotland Yard. It did not seem to matter. The brief period of exhilaration had been short-lived; she felt far worse than she had before. It wasn't because of Rollison but because of the evidence she now possessed that this might be—this *was*—dangerous. She glanced up to the next landing and could just see Mrs Tirrell, who hadn't moved.

If she should die—

Judith opened the door and Jolly removed his hat, revealing thin, grey hair. In a brief glance she studied his face: it was part of her work to study faces and she did so subconsciously. He looked a gloomy man; his pale face was heavily lined and beneath the chin were many sagging wrinkles, as if he had once been much fatter; now he was thin and looked a little frail. He had doe-like brown eyes and when he smiled at her it was with a touch of eagerness merging with anxiety.

'Miss Lorne?'

'Yes; do come in.'

He passed her but was facing her as she closed the door. She was used to tension now and recognised it in his manner.

'There's been—' she began and then stopped, for 'accident' seemed the wrong word.

He raised a hand, as if to ward off some sudden rush of fear and she added hastily: 'It's all right now, except that—'

'Is Mr Rollison still here?'

'Oh, yes!'

'I shouldn't worry, Miss Lorne, whatever the trouble is,' said Jolly. His voice was soft and reassuring and his smile was friendly and warming; fear had gone. 'Mr Rollison will look after everything.'

'Wrong,' said Rollison, from the front-room door. 'You'll look after everything, Jolly. The police and an ambulance will be here in a few minutes. Miss Lorne will tell you what happened. You'll stay with the injured woman until the police arrive. The moment they come take them up to Miss Lorne's flat and tell them a dangerous customer is in the kitchen— a man who's lost his gun but might use a kitchen chopper.'

That was the moment when Jolly said the thing which made Judith gasp—and then laugh. Her reaction was absurd but she couldn't help herself. She laughed weakly and leaned against the wall while Rollison pressed her hand and Jolly opened the door for him.

Jolly had said, 'Very good, sir.'

*   *   *

It was nearly a quarter to five when Rollison left the house in Knoll Road. As he turned the corner into a long street leading to a main road a police car swung round and Rollison had to pull sharply into the kerb. He smiled sweetly at the police-car driver who ignored him and raced towards Number 23.

*   *   *

'Now,' murmured Rollison: 'I must hurry.'

He spoke to himself as he turned on to the Embankment where traffic was thin but would soon get congested for the roads would be thronged with home-going workers from the City and the West End.

He ignored the thirty-miles-an-hour limit, cursed at every traffic light that turned red against him, slid past other cars and cut in with an abandon which brought many protests and drew dark scowls from at least two

44

policemen. He drew near the Houses of Parliament and the Abbey, swept along the wide road between them, swung round Parliament Square and was lucky with the traffic. He reached Westminster Bridge, which was already thronged with pedestrians, and was forced to slow down by a line of trams and traffic several cars deep; if the luck went against him, this would become a serious traffic-block. He glanced towards the Thames on the left and saw the two big buildings of Scotland Yard, one white, one red; he smiled. Then the traffic began to move again.

He had a good run to Cannon Street; then met more dense traffic and felt an increasing sense of frustration as he crawled behind an empty lorry. London's narrow, twisting streets prevented speed and he was in a desperate hurry, although he did not quite know why. There was nothing tangible in the evidence— except the implication that the message to Judith had been in the form of a suicide note. The note was evidence the police would be sure to find and could easily be accepted as a confession. Already the police and the public believed Mellor to be a murderer; and it had been an ugly, brutal murder. There would be no compassion for the killer once he was found.

Rollison knew the East End well. He slipped along East Cheap, with broken buildings and empty sites on either side, the pavements thronged with office-workers who had grown used to the desolation of bombing and scurried past to bus and train. At Tower Hill he swung towards the approach to Tower Bridge, was held up for three minutes and felt almost as much on edge as Judith Lorne had felt. Then he had a clear run and his knowledge of the mean, twisting streets became important.

Asham Street was near the river—and near the Red Lion. If you knew your East End, you knew your pubs. This was an old one with a wall shored up by heavy timbers because dozens of houses on one side had been blasted out of existence during the war. He remembered coming here the day after the raid and seeing the *'Beer as Usual'* sign chalked on a board perched on the rubble. He drove past the red doors of the pub and saw a young man, carrying an attaché case, on the other side of the road.

He pulled up.

'Hop in,' he said and leaned across and opened the door. 'All quiet?'

Snub Higginbottom got in, jammed the corner of his case against Rollison's arm, said 'Sorry' and grinned. He was a young man to whom smiling came easily. He had a merry face and a snub nose, fair, rather curly hair and a genial ugliness which most men and nearly all women found attractive.

'No one's thrown any bombs or broken any

windows and I haven't had my face pushed in. Expecting trouble?'

'I don't know.'

'That sounds lovely and ominous,' said Snub and pushed the case over into the back of the car. 'That's just for show,' he said. 'If you have a case you presumably have some business in these 'ere parts. I wouldn't like to be a rent collector around here, would you? What's she like?'

'Too good for you.'

'All that her photograph promised?'

'She's all right,' said Rollison. 'She had a note which was phoney and makes me think that Mellor might be about ready for the high jump. He's at Number 51—or that's what I'm told.'

'Might have been sold a pup, eh?'

'Well, it's possible. I once gave you a job.'

Rollison slid the car to a standstill outside Number 43 and climbed out. He glanced up and down the street and, although no one was in sight, knew that he was observed; no one driving this year's model in Asham Street would be ignored. It was a long, narrow, dreary street with tiny houses packed closely together on either side. All the houses looked exactly the same—a drab grey, like the pavement and the road. At intervals were grey-painted lamp-posts, the only things which broke the dreary line of desolation.

Each house had three floors; each front door

opened on to the street and led to a narrow passage and a narrow flight of stairs. Most of the small front windows were covered with lace curtains, many frayed, some of them dirty; but here and there the curtains were fresh and bright and in the window of Number 49 was a bowl of blazing scarlet tulips.

'What have you done to your hand?' asked Snub.

'I was bitten by a dog.'

'Mad dog?'

'At the moment probably insane but with any luck he's cooling off in a police cell.'

'You are a one,' said Snub—and when Rollison paused outside the door of Number 51, without a smile enlivening the grimness of his expression, Snub frowned. 'Sorry. Expect violence?'

'I've told you I don't know what to expect. Try the front door, will you?'

'I could hop round the back,' suggested Snub.

'Later, maybe.'

Snub tried the front door and found it locked. At the window of the front room a curtain, more grey than white, moved as if stirred by the wind but the window was tightly closed.

'Watching eyes,' muttered Snub. 'Ought we to be together?'

Rollison lifted the brass knocker which hadn't been cleaned for days and was dull and green, spotted with verdigris. The sound of his knocking echoed up and down the street. Two men, one young, one very old, cycled past, staring at both the men and the car.

Shuffling footsteps sounded inside the hall.

'Get back a bit,' said Rollison.

Snub stood three yards away from him, wary and watchful. The lock clicked and the door opened a few inches. Rollison saw a slatternly old woman with thin grey hair in curlers. She clutched the neck of her drab black dress.

'Yes, wot is it?' Her voice squeaked.

'I've come to see your lodger,' Rollison said. 'It's all right, Ma.' He slipped a pound-note out of his pocket and rustled it. The door opened and a skinny hand shot out. Rollison put his foot against the door, to prevent it from being closed in his face. 'A young fellow who hasn't been here long. Is he in?'

'You ain't a copper, are you?'

'Did you ever know a copper who paid for information in pound notes?'

'*Notes*?'

He laughed, added another pound and held both lightly.

'Is he in?'

'Yeh.'

'Alone?'

'Yeh.'

'Which room?'

'Top, right.'

He gave her the two pounds and said: 'Go

back into your room, Ma.'

She looked at him through thin lashes with watery, bleary eyes and shuffled into the front room. A stale smell of vegetables and dampness met Rollison who thrust the door wide open and looked up the stairs. He paused. Nothing happened, no one appeared. He beckoned Snub who came in and closed the door, making the passage dark. Rollison called:

'Mellor!'

A clock with a tinny bell struck the half-hour.

Rollison reached the foot of the stairs and peered upwards, then began to mount. Snub stayed behind, still watchful but he knew that Rollison did not really expect an attack, was afraid only of what he might find here. The stairs creaked under Rollison's light tread, the landing boards groaned.

Rollison went up the next flight and tapped on the door to the right. There was no answer. He tried the handle and pushed the door but it was locked. He pushed it again, frowning. Doors in this type of house were of flimsy wood and shook and rattled under pressure— but this one was curiously tight fitting.

Snub whispered: 'All okay?'

'Stay there,' Rollison called back.

He took out a pen-knife, one of the blades of which was a skeleton key, and inserted that blade into the lock. It was an easy lock to pick

50

but his hand was painful and the handkerchief got in the way. He took it off. The teeth marks showed clearly but only the two canine teeth had broken the skin.

The lock clicked back.

Rollison pushed but the door stuck. He pushed again, the door swung open and gas rushed out at him.

CHAPTER FIVE

'The Doc'

Snub came racing up the stairs as Rollison held his breath and rushed into the room. The gas was like an invisible blanket through which he had to force his way. He saw Mellor lying on the floor with his face near the gas-fire and heard the gentle hissing.

Behind him, Snub started coughing.

Rollison turned off the gas, reached the window and saw the flock padding round the sides. He bent his elbow and crashed it through the glass. Then he took out his cigarette-case, shielded his face with one hand and smashed the pieces which stuck out round the sides in spiteful, pointed spikes. The splintering of glass merged with Snub's coughing. The inrush of air made Rollison begin to cough but he finished his job before he gave way to it.

Snub wasn't in the room now.

Rollison leaned against the wall, doubled up with the paroxysm, his eyes streaming. Mellor's face was blurred but a pinky colour. He lay on his side with a pillow beneath his head, his knees bent naturally; he looked as if he were asleep.

Snub came in with a handkerchief tied round his mouth and nose, his eyes bright above it. Rollison pointed at Mellor, went to the window and breathed in the clean, fresh air, held his breath and turned round to help. Snub was lifting Mellor but the dead weight was too much for him. Rollison helped and felt as if his chest were bursting but they got the man on to the landing.

A shrill voice sounded.

'Wot are you doin' of? Eh? Wot are you doin' of?'

Snub's voice was muffled beneath the wet handkerchief.

'Get him on to my shoulder; I can manage.'

He went down three stairs. Rollison hoisted Mellor up a little, Snub twisted round until the unconscious man was over his shoulder, turned unsteadily and went downstairs. Rollison returned to the room and began to cough again; it would take a long time for the gas to clear. He saw the blue sheet of paper and the screwed-up envelope, put them in his pocket and, coughing painfully, went out.

'Answer me, can't yer?'

'The police will answer you,' Snub said sharply. 'Open the door.'

A draught of air swept upwards as the front door opened. Rollison went down and the old woman stood in the doorway, her fists clenched, eyes glaring with fright. Rollison touched her on the shoulder and she spun round. There was fear in her eyes because she knew what had happened to the pink-faced man who was hanging like a corpse over Snub's shoulder.

Rollison said: 'If the police come, don't tell them that the Toff called.'

'The—*torf*?' She caught her breath.

'If they don't come, just keep your mouth shut about everything,' Rollison said.

He pushed past her, into the street. Farther along, Snub was lifting Mellor into the back seat of the Rolls-Bentley; by the time Rollison arrived, he was getting into the driving-seat. He had taken off the handkerchief and had it in his hand. Two men and a young woman walked past, eyeing them curiously; two or three children stood and watched; there were faces at many of the windows. The silent spectators heard the engine start up but didn't hear Snub say:

'Nearest hospital?'

'No. The clinic.'

'Oh, sure.'

As the car moved off, the children ran

53

towards it and brushed their fingers along the shiny green wings, poking out their tongues at the driver. The old woman at Number 51 slammed the door. They drove swiftly down Asham Street towards the docks. They could see the masts of shipping and the gaunt outline of cranes at the quayside above the countless roof-tops and the pencil-slim chimneys. At the end Snub turned left into another long, narrow road. The same kind of houses were on either side but this road twisted and turned. Farther along great warehouses with grey brick walls rose up against the sky.

A police constable on a bicycle turned a corner.

He stared at the car, slowed down—and then raised his hand in salute. Rollison forced a smile for he had been recognised and if he didn't acknowledge the salute the constable would wonder why and might ask questions of the local copper's nark.

He was still feeling a little sick.

Snub said: 'Think the Doc will play?'

'Yes.'

The car purred along the winding street, forced to slow down as two horse-drawn drays came out of the gateway leading to a warehouse. Two turnings to the left and they came to a road along a wharf with ships on one side and a pub, painted bright red, on the corner; above the pub, starkly outlined against the hazy sky, was a huge red lion. Not far along this street was a large, corrugated-iron shed; alongside it several Nissen huts. The whole area had been razed during the bombing and these were temporary buildings. Beyond them row after row of prefabricated houses, like pale white boxes, made a slight change in the drab scene. Dozens of men and women walked or cycled along this road, many more than there had been in Asham Street.

The tin building and the huts were surrounded by a wire fence and the double gates were open. Snub turned the car into it and pulled up in front of one of the huts. A huge signboard carried the word MEDICAL CLINIC and beneath them the hours of attendance. A nurse in neat uniform came out of the big building and looked curiously at the car.

'I wish it were dark,' said Rollison.

'Have a slice of the moon,' Snub said. 'We aren't going to get away with this one; the Doc won't play.'

He got out and, as he approached the Nissen hut, the door opened and a middle-aged man appeared. He looked burly in an old tweed suit with baggy trousers and bulging pockets.

He had a round, ruddy face and a frizzy grey head, bald at the top.

Rollison called: 'Emergency, Doc. You may need oxygen. Coal-gas poisoning.'

The doctor pursed his lips, as if in

55

disapproval, turned and disappeared.

Snub had the back of the car open and eased Mellor out. His face was still pink-tinged, his eyes were closed, he didn't seem to be breathing.

'*Corpus*,' Snub murmured.

They carried him between them into the Nissen hut and the doctor called out:

'In here, Rollison.'

He stood in a small room where there were two empty beds, painted with green enamel, covered with sheets and blankets. The room was spotlessly clean. Several pieces of apparatus stood about it including an oxygen cylinder, stand and equipment, by the head of one of the beds. Snub and Rollison put Mellor down and the doctor said:

'Collar, shoes and belt loosened, quickly. You ought to have undone them before. Close the door, will you?'

He spoke in a quiet, unflurried voice with a slight north-country accent and went unhurriedly about his business, sparing time even to look hard and long at Rollison.

'Press down that top switch by the bed, will you? Electric blanket,' he added. After a pause: 'If you'd given me a ring, I could have had it all ready.'

He put on a long white coat.

'Sorry,' said Rollison.

'My wife's in the kitchen,' said the doctor. 'Get her to make some coffee, will you? Have a strong cup yourself.'

'I'll stay, thanks,' said Rollison. 'Snub, pop along and be nice to Mrs Willerby.'

Snub went out, closing the door carefully behind him, and the doctor turned from the oxygen mask and bag which he was fixing over Mellor's face. 'Well, Doc?'

'Asking for miracles again?'

'He isn't dead—or he wasn't.'

'No. I think we might pull him round. That's not the miracle I was talking about.'

Rollison smiled. 'I get you. Yes, I'm asking for miracles again.'

'Who is he?'

'You'd better not know.'

'Hmm. If we do save him, what do you want?'

'I'll look after that if you'll keep him here for the night and attend to him when he's moved. I don't want anyone to know that he's alive. In fact—' He paused and shrugged his shoulders. 'The less you know the better, Doc.'

'Is he wanted?'

'Yes but if they tried him, he would get off—or should. If I can stall for a bit while I look round I think I can save him from trial.'

'*Hmm*!' There was a ghost of a twinkle in the keen grey eyes. 'You don't change much. Did he do this gassing job himself?'

'I don't know and you don't know.'

'Who does know anything?' asked the doctor.

57

He was fitting a stethoscope to his ears and bending over Mellor's bare pink chest.

'No one who'll talk, as far as I can judge. If anyone does talk, I'll confess I hoodwinked you and keep you in the clear.'

'That's what you think. Don't forget I'm not the free agent I used to be. I'm a servant of the Government and so a servant of the State, who run the police.'

'That man's a human being, in a nasty spot of trouble.'

The doctor shrugged his shoulders and turned his full attention on to the patient. He kept frowning as he shifted the stethoscope, finally shook his head, stood up, let the listening piece fall against his chest and opened a drawer in a small table. He took out a hypodermic syringe and selected a tiny glass phial. The care with which he prepared it all fascinated Rollison.

'I'm going to give him an intravenous injection,' the doctor said. 'Then we'd better see how much saturation there is. Any idea how long he's been unconscious?'

'No.'

'Pity. Shift him a bit, will you? and take care not to let the mask slip. Then see if you can get his left arm out of his coat sleeve and roll the shirt sleeve up.' The doctor worked all the time and went on talking in the same unflurried voice. 'The trouble with you, Rollison, is that you're always a man with a

58

mission. Nothing matters but getting results. You'd have made a good pirate—you've the buccaneering way with you. Yes, you were born three hundred years too late. As it is, this is a disciplined and orderly world.'

'Really,' said Rollison sardonically.

'And you're always kicking against the discipline,' said the doctor. He glowered up at Rollison who had Mellor's arm out of his coat and was rolling up a grubby shirt sleeve. The arm was limp and pink. 'You always have. The police have never been quick enough or thorough enough for you—you've always had to get a step in front of them and show them the way. Or think you're showing them the way. I doubt if they agree. Why not let the police know all about this young man and save yourself a lot of bother?'

'It's the buccaneer in me.'

'I'm serious.'

'I'll be serious. Ninety-nine times in a hundred the police do a good job—a much more effective job than I could hope to do. But every now and again a peculiar case crops up. This is one. Apply rules and regulations to this and you'll be in danger of reaching what the world thinks is a right and proper verdict; in fact it would be a travesty. Give rules and regulations the go-by for a bit and you'll get justice.'

'And you're all for justice!'

'Who's been giving you a pep talk?' asked

59

Rollison.

The doctor was rubbing spirit into the crook of Mellor's elbow and the faint, sharp smell was refreshing.

'I'm giving you the pep,' said the doctor. 'Hold his arm out, will you? Keep it limp.' He picked up the hypodermic syringe. 'Can you honestly tell me that if you keep Mellor away from the police it will help him—and help to find Galloway's murderer?' He smiled again at Rollison's startled expression and said with gentle reproof: 'Keep his arm still—I've got to get this into the vein slowly. Well, can you?'

'So you know who he is,' murmured Rollison slowly.

'Even doctors have eyes and he's been on the wanted list for weeks. I don't have to talk about it but before I help I want to be fairly sure that this isn't one of your crazy revolts against an orderly society—that it will be a wise thing to hide him from the police for a little longer. Convince me and I'll do what I can.'

The doctor began to press the plunger, gently, and kept his eye on a large clock which ticked away the seconds as he made the injection.

CHAPTER SIX

Bill Ebbutt

The hypodermic syringe was empty before Rollison spoke. The doctor drew the needle out gently, wiped it on a piece of cotton wool and stood back to survey the patient. Footsteps sounded outside and there was a tap at the door. The doctor turned to open it and Snub came in with two cups of steaming coffee on a tray, some milk, sugar and biscuits. He flashed an inquiring glance at Rollison who showed no expression.

'Anything else?' asked Snub.

'Yes,' said Rollison. 'Telephone Bill Ebbutt and tell him I want a room for a stranger— probably for a couple of weeks. The stranger will want nursing for the first few days.'

'Nice work. Thanks, Doc.' Snub went out.

The doctor rubbed the side of his face. He had a broad nose, a full mouth, a squarish chin which seemed to be a little on one side. His white collar was a shade too tight but that didn't seem to trouble him.

'That young man isn't the only one who jumped to conclusions,' he said.

'You said you'd play if I could convince you,' said Rollison. 'I can—you'll play. Mellor is the illegitimate son of an extremely wealthy old

61

man. The old man has been suffering from heart trouble for some years. Recently, in spite of strict obedience to doctor's orders, he has become much worse. The doctors say they're puzzled. I'm not. He's worse because someone is working on him. I suspected jiggery-pokery shortly after he asked me to look for his son. There is quite a story behind this. He also had a legitimate son, Geoffrey, a year younger than Mellor. The younger son was burned to death, supposedly by accident, nearly a year ago. The fire was in a summer-house where Geoffrey slept in warm weather. He would have inherited the bulk of a substantial fortune. After his death, conscience set to work in the old man who decided that if he could find his first son, he would do right by him. As they say.' Rollison's expression didn't change and he looked at the doctor through the haze of steam rising from the coffee. 'That's the story as I know it.'

'Go on.'

'Inquiries were made discreetly. Mellor had no idea that he was a rich man's son, no idea that the rich man was waiting to present him with a fortune. But someone knew. The someone framed Mellor for Galloway's murder. I've been through the evidence thoroughly and had counsel's opinion and counsel's opinion is that nothing except fresh evidence can prevent Mellor from being hanged. I've some fresh evidence but it isn't complete yet. If the police get it, there's a grave risk that they'll let whoever is behind the crimes know that they're on a new trail. Two possibilities arise from that, Doc. Either the crooks will get a move on and the old man will die very quickly—an attempt at a *coup d'état*, as it were. Or else they'll lie low, covering up their tracks, let justice take its course with Mellor—great joke, isn't it?—and nature take its course with the old man. Eventually, whoever wants the fortune will probably get it. It's certainly someone who's in line for it. The chance of finding the whole truth will be very slim. Or it would have been but for a thing that happened to-day. The crooks clearly wanted to get a move on, something worried them into making a mistake. Mind if I go all egotistic?'

'You worried them—I'll believe that!'

'Thanks. I think they discovered that I'd discovered that Mellor was this long-lost son. So they made a hasty move and also their first major mistake. I think I can now prove that they were prepared to murder Mellor and that alone would cast some doubt and bring new evidence. But they also showed something else. This is not what it looked like in the first place—simply a nasty domestic business with an avaricious next-but-one-of-kin getting rid of the but-one. I won't say this is gangster stuff but some pretty hardened bad men are involved. If the police take Mellor these

63

gentlemen will know exactly where they stand. If Mellor disappears again they'll be at sixes and sevens and they'll do more desperate things to find him.'

'*Hmm*,' grunted the doctor. 'And you'll stick your neck right out.'

'That's it.'

'Well, if the police don't ask me whether I've seen Mellor, I won't tell them,' said the doctor. 'If they ask whether I've seen you, I shall tell them all about it.'

'I hope they don't ask until I've got Mellor away from here. When can he be moved?'

'To-morrow, at the earliest. You'll have to arrange for an ambulance or a shooting-brake—I don't want him jolted about too much, even to-morrow. And of course he may not pull through,' added the doctor. 'In that case—'

'The show's over,' said Rollison. 'But he'll pull through. Thank you, Doc.'

'No one can help being born a fool,' said the doctor. 'I'll give him another quarter of an hour and if he isn't showing signs of improvement by then I'll have to do a blood test. There's no need for you to wait. I'll telephone you when I can be sure which way he'll turn. Get my wife to dress that bite in your hand before you go and give my love to the other buccaneer.'

Rollison looked puzzled. 'The other one?'

The doctor chuckled, and said: 'Bill Ebbutt.

Who else? Tell him I said so, won't you?'

*   *   *

To the stranger passing through there is only a drab greyness in the East of London, relieved here and there by garish brightness in the shops, at the cinemas and the more prosperous public-houses. Rollison, who knew the district well, saw beyond the surface to the heart of the East End, knew its colour and gaiety, its careless generosity, its pulsating life.

The district had grown upon him over the years until it was to him the real heart of London and the West End was a city apart. When he had first come he had been full of the impetuosity of youth, a born adventurer seeking adventure and seeking criminals at the same time. Then he had believed the East End to be a haunt of vice, had seen almost every man as a potential criminal. He had discovered that the East Enders presented a solid front against the police, an iron curtain behind which lawlessness prevailed. But even that was false. The curtain was there, thick, almost impenetrable. There remained parts of the East End where policemen always went in pairs because it was dangerous for them to patrol the streets alone. But the great majority of the people had no more to do with crime than the great masses in the dormitory suburbs; less than many in the West End.

Their distrust of the police was born of what they considered injustice; from the days when the police had harassed and pestered them about petty, insignificant misdemeanours; from the days, in fact, when a man could be hanged for stealing a lamb and when sheep had grazed within easy distance of the East End, easy for the taking by hungry folk.

Over the years a kind of wary armistice had sprung up between the East Enders and the police. The curtain remained but was less thick, less formidable.

Rollison had penetrated beyond the curtain when it had been discovered that he bore no malice against small-part crooks but had a burning hatred for murderers, blackmailers, white-slavers, dope-runners—the motley collection of rogues who gathered for their own protection behind the curtain, emerging only to raid the West End or the provinces, then sneaking back. There was no love lost between the average Cockney and these parasites; nor was there betrayal for they had a common enemy: the law.

After a while Rollison had made friends with many East Enders and among the first was Bill Ebbutt. It was said that Ebbutt had first nicknamed him 'The Toff.' Whoever it had been, the soubriquet had stuck. Many people would look blank if they heard the name Rollison but would relax and nod genially when 'The Toff' was mentioned. For he did much for them quietly, often anonymously, and did not hesitate to take up their cause even if it were unpopular. So he was accepted by most and hated by some—the real criminals, the gang-leaders, the vice kings.

Sometimes fear of what the Toff might do led to a widespread campaign to discredit him in the East End; once or twice it had come near to success. It might happen again but, as he drove from the clinic to Bill Ebbutt's place, Rollison did not think it would happen for a long time.

He did know that already the whisper of his latest visit was spreading, in rooms, houses, pubs, billiards-saloons, doss-houses, warehouses, shops and factories, throughout the docks and along the Thames and the Thames-side. A simple, good-humoured whisper, creating the same kind of feeling that came when you went to bed with the knowledge that you would awaken to a fine, bright day. He would have been less than human had it not pleased him.

*   *   *

Bill Ebbutt was a massive man, getting on in years and showing it physically but with a mind as keen and alert as it had ever been. He was a connoisseur of beers and ales; of boxing; and of invective. Of these three, he loved boxing most. That was why he, some years earlier, from the high state of landlord of the Blue Dog, had become the sole owner of *Bill Ebbutt's Gymnasium*. This was behind the pub—a large, square wooden building with a corrugated-iron roof and it looked rather like the clinic. The entrance faced a side street. There were always several old men standing about, smoking their pipes or chewing their *Old Nod*, waiting for opening time when they could wet their whistles on beer which had to be good to be sold in the Blue Dog.

Inside the wooden building a huge room was fitted up as a gymnasium which would not have disgraced a public school or a leading professional football club. Parallel bars, ropes, vaulting-horses, punch-balls, chest-expanders, locked rowing machines—all the impedimenta of a gymnasium were there. In addition there were two rings, one at each end—the second ring was a recent installation, Bill's latest pride. In the farthest corner from the door a little room was partitioned off and outside was a single word: *Office*, printed badly and fading. Bill was the most approachable man in the world when outside but, ensconced in the tiny, over-crowded and over-heated office, the walls of which were covered with photographs of his young hopes or his champions wearing prize belts, he was as difficult of access as a dictator.

At nearly half-past six that day he was alone in the office, poring over a copy of *Sporting*

Life. He was wearing glasses and was still ashamed of it—that was one of the reasons why he hated anyone to come in. They were large and horn-rimmed and gave his ugly, battered face with its one cauliflower ear and its flattened nose the look of a professorial chimpanzee. His lips were pursed. Occasionally he parted them to emit a slow, deliberate term of abuse. Sometimes he would start and peer closer at the tiny print, as if he could not believe what was written there. Occasionally, too, he clenched his massive fist and thumped the table which served as his desk.

'*The blistering son of a festering father,*' he breathed and thumped. 'The pig-eyed baboon. I'll turn 'is 'ead rahnd so 'e don't know wevver 'e's comin' or goin'. *The flickin' fraud*, I'll burn 'im.'

There was a tap at the door.

'Go a-*way!*' he roared without lifting his head. '*The perishin', lyin', 'alf-baked son've a nape.* No boy o' mine ever won a a fairer fight. To say 'e won on a foul—'

There was another tap.

'I told yer to 'op it! 'Op it, or I'll slit yer gizzard, yer mangy ape. Look wot 'e says abaht the *ref*. Strike a light! I'll tear 'im to pieces. I—'

The man outside was persistent but the third tap had a lighter sound, as if timidity had intervened.

69

'*Go an' fry yerself!*' Bill slid off his chair. 'Why, if I 'ave ter tell yer again—'

'Bill, look aht,' came a plaintive whisper. 'She's just comin' in. Don't say I didn't warn yer.'

'I'll break 'im up inter small pieces an roast 'im. The ruddy, lyin', effin'—'

The door swung open and a diminutive woman dressed in tight, old-fashioned clothes with a flowering skirt which almost reached her ankles and a wide-brimmed straw hat in which two feathers, scarlet and yellow, bobbed fiercely, entered the office. Bill started and snatched off his glasses.

'So you're still at it,' said the woman, her mouth closing like a trap as she finished the sentence. 'You know where you'll end up, don't yer? You'll end up in 'ell.'

'I don't want none of your fire-an'-brimstone talk, Lil,' growled Ebbutt. 'If you'd seen the way they've torn the Kid apart, you'd want ter tear a strip orf 'em yerself.' His tone was conciliatory and his manner almost as timid as the third warning tap. 'Wotjer want?'

'I thought you would like to know, Mr Ebbutt, that a certain gentleman is going to pay us a visit,' said Bill's wife, in a tone of practised refinement.

'I don't want ter see no one, unless it's that perishin' boxing correspondent. Then I'd—'

'I will tell Mr Rollison,' said Lil, and turned on her high heels.

70

Ebbutt blinked. ' 'Oo? 'Ere! Come orf it, Lil; 'ave a n'eart, duck. Is Mr Ar arahnd?'

'I thought you was only interested in boxers,' said Lil with a sniff.

Ebbutt slipped his arm round her waist. Standing together, his mountainous figure dwarfed her lath-like slimness. They were in the open doorway. A few youngsters were training, one smiting a punch-ball as if it were a mortal enemy and another doing a series of somersaults. Round the walls lounged men in shabby clothes and no one appeared to take any notice of the Ebbutts.

'Take it easy, Lil. Do me a power of good, Mr Ar would. No one I'd rather 'ave a chat wiv.'

'And I suppose I ought to feel *h*onoured,' snapped Lil.

'Come orf it.' Ebbutt squeezed her waist and she looked up at him with a quick, teasing smile.

'That 'Igginbottom rang up,' she told him. 'You was engaged at the office, so he got through to the pub apartment. Mr Rollison's coming to see you and he wants a room ready for a stranger.'

'Gor blimey! Wot's 'e up to?'

'I expect he'll tell you, when it suits him,' said Lil. 'Wants a nurse, too. It looks as if someone's in trouble. I told Mr 'Igginbottom I would arrange all that was necessary, I was sure you wouldn't have no time. Annie will

71

take him in.'

Ebbutt scratched his chin.

'Annie's okay. Not a bad idea, Lil, ta. Where are you goin', all toffed up?'

Lil drew herself from his grasp, gave her coat a pat and bobbed her feathers.

'You can find me at the *H*army Social,' she said. 'And I don't want to find you drunk when I get home.'

Ebbutt didn't wait to see her royal progress across the gymnasium, passing the men who stopped what they were doing and touched their forelocks or smiled and, according to their social status, called her Lil or Mrs Ebbutt. Nor did he wait to see the amused grins which followed her into the street. He went back into the small office, folded up *Sporting Life*, forgetful of his rage against the boxing correspondent, and sat down to wonder what the Toff wanted now. He was fiddling with his glasses when a diminutive man wearing a grey polo sweater and a pair of razor-creased yellow trousers sidled into the room and coughed.

Ebbutt looked down at him amiably.

'Mr Ar's comin' to 'ave a look rahnd, Charlie. Git everyfing nice an' tidy, woncha?'

'Okay,' said Charlie. 'Proper day for visitors, ain't it, Bill? First the missus, then Mr Ar and now the busies.'

Ebbutt started. 'Busies? 'Oo said so?'

'I say so. Gricey's just coming in.'

With the door open, it was possible to see the entrance to the gymnasium and on the wall opposite the door was a mirror, placed askew and apparently without any significance. Ebbutt glanced into it; the gymnasium entrance was reflected there. He saw a man's shadow, then the man himself. It was Superintendent Grice of New Scotland Yard.

He said in a whisper: 'Send some boys aht, Charlie. Tell Mr Ar 'oo's 'ere, quick. It wouldn't s'prise me if they ain't arter the same fing and I wouldn't like the Torf to run inter Gricey if 'e don't wanter see 'im. Look slippy!'

'Oke.' Charlie slid out of the office. Grice caught sight of him and shook his fist playfully. Charlie said: 'Nice ter see yer, Mr Grice,' and went past him.

Grice, a tall, spare man, dressed in brown with brown hair and a sallow skin stretched tightly across his face, making the bridge of his nose seem white, reached the office door while Ebbutt was ostensibly studying a racing-form chart. Grice tapped heavily on the wall and Ebbutt started.

'Why, if it ain't Mr Grice!'

'Isn't this a nice surprise?' asked Grice, coming in. 'I suppose you've sent Charlie out for some ice-cream.' He hitched up a leather-topped stool and sat on it. 'Or has he gone out to warn Rollison?'

73

CHAPTER SEVEN

Friendly Advice

'Don't look now,' said Snub, 'but I think that chap with the battered titfer has recognised you.'

A little man wearing a trilby with a shapeless brim stood at the side of the road, waving wildly towards the car. Rollison slowed down and pulled towards him. They were a few minutes away from the gymnasium and not far from the Mile End Road. The hum of traffic was loud, the street was crowded.

'Hallo, Percy,' greeted Rollison.

'Nice ter see yer, Mr Ar. Bill told me ter keep a look aht for yer.'

'Why?'

'Gricey's just gone inter see 'im.'

'Oh,' said Rollison. 'Grice hasn't lost much time.'

'Bill thought yer might prefer not to run inter 'im,' said Percy, a man with an ugly face, a friendly smile and teeth stained through chewing tobacco. 'Gricey was on 'is own; it ain't often 'e runs arahnd wivvout a bodyguard, is it?'

'This must be just a social call,' said Rollison. 'Going back to the gym, Percy?'

'Yeh!'

74

'Hop in the back. Snub'—Rollison touched the youngster's arm—'I think you'd better scram. Go to Knoll Road and, if Judith's still there, take her to the flat as soon as you can. If there's any reason why she has to stay at her own place, stay with her.'

'Suits me,' said Snub.

'That's nice for you,' Rollison said and, as Snub jumped out, drove off again.

Percy sat perched forward on the seat so that every passer-by could see that he was riding in state. Rollison drove swiftly to the gymnasium where many more than the usual dozen or so loungers were waiting. He knew that every one of them was aware that the great Grice was in the East End.

Grice, one of the Big Five at the Yard, knew the East End well; all the East End knew him. He had spent years at AZ Division, had been a terror in his youth—but fair in all he did. If a single policeman was liked in this district, it was Grice; but even he was regarded with suspicion. Usually he came to the East End with Divisional men because he wouldn't break the unwritten police law and come alone on real business; so this was an unofficial call.

A dozen men called out cheerfully to Rollison as he left the car. He smiled right and left, feeling curiously at home in spite of the contrast between the luxury of the car and the dinginess of the district and between his

75

clothes and theirs. He stepped into the gloomy gymnasium and saw the office door wide open. Charlie stood outside one of the rings where two light-weights pranced about.

Charlie jerked his head towards the office.

'Thanks,' said Rollison.

He knew why the mirror was in that particular place and that Grice was also aware of it. So he made no attempt to take the Yard man by surprise. Grice, still sitting on the stool with his hands in his pockets, looked round with a grin. Ebbutt took off his glasses.

'Why, fancy seein' you, Mr Ar!'

'Yes, fancy,' said Grice. 'Hallo, Rolly.'

Rollison gravely shook hands with Ebbutt. Grice kept his hands in his pockets. The flapping sound of gloves hitting gloves stopped and they knew that the far doorway was crowded, everyone was trying to see what was happening in the office.

'On holiday?' Rollison asked Grice.

'Just taking an hour off.'

'And hundreds of bad men are running around London doing what they like,' reproached Rollison. 'Give the ratepayer a square deal, old chap.'

'Cor!' choked Ebbutt. 'Cor, that's a good one, that is!' He was doubled up, not altogether with mirth but to hide his confusion, for he was on edge and embarrassed. 'Cor, that's wunnerful, Mr Ar!'

'Yes, isn't he good?' asked Grice dryly. 'You

76

on holiday, Rolly, or just looking for trouble?'

'Your guess,' said Rollison.

Grice shrugged. 'I don't have to guess; I know. I thought I'd probably find you here and I've come on a mission of good will.'

'The improbable policeman,' murmured Rollison.

'Did you find Mellor?' asked Grice and leaned back on the stool, looking at Rollison through his lashes.

Ebbutt grunted as if something had struck him in the stomach and shot a glance at Rollison, whose poker-face gave nothing away.

'It's still your guess,' he said.

'I don't want to waste time guessing. Rolly, I know you're full of good intentions and we've done some useful work together but be careful. Mellor is a killer.'

'So you say.'

'I know he's a killer. There isn't any argument about it. He's not worth your attention.'

'Judge and jury both, are you?' asked Rollison.

'Where is he?' demanded Grice.

'You've been after him for a month. Don't you know?'

Grice frowned. 'So it's like that? I was afraid of it when I heard you'd been to see Judith Lorne. She's a nice kid and I know you've a soft spot for damsels in distress but you'd be

77

wise to convince her gently that she got tied up with a bad 'un and she ought to forget him. That's the simple truth of it. Why didn't you come and see me if you thought you had something on Mellor?'

'I didn't think we'd see eye to eye.'

'If you're going to campaign for Mellor, we won't.'

'That's too bad because I'm campaigning for him. But we don't have to quarrel.'

'I think we shall have to if you're awkward.' Grice didn't shift his position. His manner was still friendly for, unlike many officers at Scotland Yard, he was well disposed towards Rollison. 'I haven't been to Knoll Road but I've heard what happened there. We picked up a man named Waleski who's charged you with common assault. His story is that you forced him out of his car at the point of a gun, made him go to Miss Lorne's flat and there knocked him about to get information from him. He says he hadn't any information he could give you, that he'd never heard of you or Miss Lorne before and he swears he'll see you in jug for this.'

Rollison laughed. 'Nice chap! Did he also mention that I held him up with his own gun and acted in self-defence?'

'Can you prove it?'

'Yes. Did he tell you that his buddy nearly killed the landlady? And is Waleski known?'

'I haven't checked very far but I don't think

78

so,' Grice said. 'Rolly, I'm serious—and you'd better listen to this, Ebbutt, because if you're not careful, Rollison will get you into trouble. The moment I knew that you'd been to see Judith Lorne I realised you were on the Mellor case. You've a clear duty. Tell us anything you may know and which we don't— I don't say there is anything but there might be—and then get out of it. It's an ugly business. Mellor may seem to you a victimised young fool but he's bad, Rolly—as bad as they come. There aren't many gangs but there are one or two bad ones. Ask Ebbutt, he'll bring you up to date. Mellor's in one of them. He's a killer. We're after him and we'd have got him if he hadn't been under cover with everyone lying themselves sick to keep him there. We're going to get Mellor eventually and we don't mind who gets hurt in the process—even if you're one of them. That's friendly advice, Rolly, and this time I think you ought to take it. Don't you, Ebbutt?'

Ebbutt grunted unintelligibly.

'He says yes,' said Grice and stood up. 'I didn't lose any time because I thought you ought to know where you stand from the beginning. You can't do anything on your own, you'll have to get the help of a lot of other people and you'll land them in a mess as well as yourself. Don't do it.' He looked down at his shoes. 'Now and again you forget what you're up against with us, you know. This ought to be an eye-opener. Fifteen minutes after my men reached Knoll Road I was talking to the AZ Division. Half an hour after that I was told you were in the East End. You can't compete with it, Rolly. If there's any way you can help us, fine—we'll be glad to listen. But if you start the lone-wolf act—'

'Heaven help me,' murmured Rollison.

'That's about it.'

'Spend another hour checking up,' advised Rollison, 'and if you can give me chapter and verse for my movements since I left Knoll Road I'll hand it to you. If you can't—lone-wolfing might have its points.'

'So it might,' agreed Grice, smiling at Ebbutt. 'He's a tough customer, isn't he? You might warn him that we could stop his act by holding him on Waleski's charge, Ebbutt. The warrant's probably been sworn. Tell him what it's like to spend a night in the cooler.'

He nodded casually and went out and the crowd near the entrance to the gymnasium broke up into ones and twos, suddenly interested only in themselves, while Bill Ebbutt fiddled with his glasses and looked like a bewildered bull. Neither he nor Rollison spoke. After Grice had driven off the flapping and punching re-started, skipping-ropes whirled, a man began to speak in short, snappy sentences, giving advice to the boys in the ring.

Then Ebbutt squared his great shoulders.

'Are you arter Mellor, Mr Ar? Is 'e the stranger? I don't mind sayin' I 'ope Gricey's got it all wrong. That Mellor's a bad lot, a real bad lot, Mr Ar.'

*   *   *

'Yes, Bill,' said Rollison. 'It's Mellor.'

Bill said awkwardly: 'I'm sorry abaht that; I am, reely.'

'Don't you feel you can hide him?'

'I don't fink I oughta, Mr Ar, that's a fack.'

'So Grice is right and I'm wrong this time.' Rollison spoke quietly without any hint of reproach.

'It ain't a question of Grice bein' right, it's wot we know abaht Mellor. If you'd 'ad a word wiv me before, Mr Ar, I could've put yer wise. That Mellor—strewth, they don't grow any worse. Anuvver of these Commando boys wot went wrong. It ain't that I blame 'em, Mr Ar, you know me; but they was brought up in a tough school, wasn't they? Taught all kinds of dirty tricks. Most of them forgot all abaht it but there's some 'oo can't forget an' like to make their money the easy way. Why didn't you arst me?' Ebbutt was almost pleading. 'I could've told yer that Mellor's a killer. Gricey's right enough abaht that. I don't 'ave to tell yer abaht Flash Dimond, do I?' He paused and, when Rollison held his peace, went on slowly: 'Now I never 'ad no time for

81

Flash. 'E was a gangster an' 'e didn't mind killin' but 'e wasn't *all* bad. 'Is gang was tough but they never went aht to kill.'

Rollison said; 'I thought Flash was dead.'

'S'right. Mellor cut 'is throat.'

'Oh,' said Rollison heavily. 'I certainly should have come to see you before, Bill; I've been away from here for too long. Are you trying to tell me that Mellor murdered Flash and took over the gang?'

'S'right.'

'And the gang's got worse?'

Ebbutt shifted his bulk from one foot to the other.

'I got to say yes, Mr Ar, I've got to say the gang's got worse. Mind yer, it ain't done so much—you never 'ear a lot abaht it. Mellor's clever. 'E pushed 'arf the gang orf. They wasn't unscrooperlous enough for him. There's abaht a dozen of them left—the worst gang in London. They don't work like a gang no longer. They do their own jobs separate but they're organised orl right. I'm telling you Gawd's trufe, Mr Ar. Remember that Kent job when the old gent got 'is 'ead bashed in and they got away wiv nine tharsand pounds worf o' sparklers? That was a Mellor job. Remember that rozzer that got 'is—shot in the guts when he questioned a coupla boys ahtside a big 'ouse? That was a Mellor job. There's been plenty an' one is worse than all the others put togevver.' Ebbutt's voice was

82

hoarse and in his earnestness he put a hand on Rollison's shoulder and pressed hard. 'There was that job at Epping. Remember? Coupla boys broke into a n'ouse where there was only a girl of twelve at 'ome. Woke 'er up an' when she started to scream, croaked 'er. *That* was a Mellor job. Mellor's aht to become the big boss. Maybe 'e'll make it. An' that's a good reason why you didn't oughter 'elp him. Sooner or later you'll come up against 'im. You always 'ave a go at gang leaders if they git too powerful. For your own sake, cut it aht, Mr Ar.'

Rollison said: 'I can't, Bill.'

Ebbutt shrugged his shoulders.

'Well, I'm afraid I can't 'elp Mellor, Mr Ar. You know wot I mean, don'tcher? It isn't anyfink against you but you ain't bin arahnd much lately, you've got a bit be'ind wiv' the news.'

Rollison said: 'So it seems. You may have got hold of the wrong end of the stick, Bill.'

Ebbutt shrugged, as if to say that he was quite certain of his facts.

'Is Mellor the kind to commit suicide?' asked Rollison.

'Nark it, Mr Ar.'

'Well, I found him, dying in front of a gas-fire that wasn't alight, Bill. I don't think it was attempted murder; I think he tried to do himself in. He may die. If he doesn't he'll be a pretty sick man and can't do any harm. And if he's the man you think he is then he's better under cover than running around loose.'

Ebbutt looked uneasy.

'If you've got Mellor, you ought ter turn 'im in,' he said. 'Sorry, Mr Ar, but that's the way I feel abaht it.'

'All right, Bill, that's the way it is.' Rollison was brisk. 'You may be right and you're certainly wise.'

'Now come orf it, Mr Ar! I'm not scared o' the dicks. If I fought there was a chance to do some good, I'd cover 'im; but—well, it's *Mellor*. If there's anyfink else I can do, I'm all for you, Mr Ar. *Anyfink*.'

Rollison smiled and clapped the old prize-fighter on the shoulder.

'I'll keep you so busy you'll feel like a spinning top. Find out if anyone has ever heard of a man named Waleski and let me know, will you? I'll write the name down.' He pulled the *Sporting Life* towards him and printed the name STANISLAS WALESKI. 'And then find out if any of the Mellor gang have turned against Mellor. Whatever he's done in the past, he's having a rough time now and he's been on the run from someone. Have you heard anything about him for the past month?'

'Not since 'e ducked,' admitted Ebbutt. 'I got to say it's a funny fing, Mr Ar. I thought 'e was sittin' pretty, waitin' for the flap to blow over.'

84

'He's been hard on the run and he's dead beat.'

'You know what these gangs are,' said Ebbutt with a shrug. ' 'E bumped Flash off; now someone else comes along an' 'as it in for 'im. Flash 'ad a lot o' friends. If you arst me, Mellor killed Galloway and the boys knew 'e'd never get away wiv it, so they turned 'im aht. That's abaht the size of it, Mr Ar. I don't mind admitting I feel bad, but—well, if the missus noo it was Mellor—'

'Don't tell her,' advised Rollison. 'Just say that the stranger isn't coming and look after the other job for me. Waleski is important. He's been staying at the Oxford Palace Hotel so he may be a newcomer. He's about five feet six, Block Jensen's build, with black eyelashes that look as if they've been stuck on. Black, heavily oiled hair with a bald patch about the size of a tea-cup. Got all that?'

'If I get a whisper you'll know abaht it, Mr Ar.'

'Thanks,' said Rollison. 'Now I'd better be off, there's a lot to do.'

*   *   *

With the police and the voice of the East End calling the same tune about Jim Mellor, it was going to be hard going. When Rollison got into the car, the group of people watching him were puzzled and silent. He looked much as

85

he had when he had tackled Waleski at Judith's flat: bleak, uncompromising, aggressive, even angry. There was a rustle of comment when he drove off, for Bill Ebbutt came to the door and watched him, but Rollison didn't glance round. So the whisper spread that there had been trouble between the Toff and Bill Ebbutt.

CHAPTER EIGHT

Neat Trick

Policemen whom Rollison passed did not salute or smile but just watched him. The change in their demeanour was so marked that he knew that word had already been spread among them, that he was to be watched and his movements reported—and that the official attitude was hostile. He drew up outside Aldgate Station, between two barrow-boys with their barrows piled up with fruit, and walked to the station entrance, making for a telephone booth. A constable saw him but took no notice until he was inside the box; then the man made a note on a pad which he took from his breast pocket.

Rollison dropped in his two pennies and dialled Doc Willerby's number. Willerby answered himself.

'How's the patient?' asked Rollison.

'He'll do,' said the doctor.

'I've heard a lot more about him than I knew before.'

'I wondered when you'd get round to that. Changed your mind?'

'No. But if you'd rather be shot of him right away, just say the word.'

'He mustn't be moved again to-night,' said Willerby. 'If the police get round to me they'll have to take over. If they don't—I don't know who the man is.'

'That's sweeter music than you know.'

'I didn't think you'd cut much ice with Mellor in the East End; Ebbutt was your only chance. Doesn't he feel buccaneer enough?'

Rollison laughed. 'Don't forget he's reformed. What's the best time to collect Mellor in the morning?'

'Before nine o'clock.'

'Right, thanks,' said Rollison. 'I'll be seeing you.'

He rang off, nodded at the constable as he stepped from the box and went more cheerfully towards his car. The interview with Ebbutt had shaken him: he had taken Ebbutt's aid for granted. He was dissatisfied with himself. He had heard of the trouble in the Dimond gang but not the name of the new leader. He had traced Mellor through his Army record and his foster-parents and had only made cursory inquiries into his post-war record. He knew that Mellor had his own small flat, played a lot of tennis and was a go-ahead manager of a small printing firm in the North-West of London.

The new information couldn't be ignored, though the Mellor he had traced seemed to be a completely different man from the Mellor Ebbutt knew. Had he stumbled upon a new Jekyll and Hyde?

When he turned into Gresham Terrace a heavily-built man was opposite Number 22g where he had his flat; the man was from the Yard although Rollison couldn't recall his name. Rollison nodded and received a blank stare in return. He let himself into the house and then went back to the pavement to survey the street and find out whether there was another Yard man about. He didn't see one.

Gresham Terrace, near Piccadilly, was a wide road with stately terraced houses on either side—a sharp contrast to the mean streets from which he had just come. The house was near a corner. Three shallow stone steps led up to a small porch. The entrance hall was long and narrow and carpeted from wall to wall. The first flight of stairs was also carpeted—the higher flights were of bare stone. He walked up thoughtfully and, when he reached the top landing which served only his flat, the door opened and Jolly appeared.

'Good evening, sir.'

'Hallo, Jolly. Everyone here?'

'Yes, sir, if you mean Miss Lorne and Mr Higginbottom.'

'I do.'

Rollison passed into the square hall, off which led all five rooms of the flat. Immediately opposite the landing was the living-room and he heard voices as that door opened and Snub beamed at him.

'All in one piece?'

'So far.'

'I say, you look a bit grimmish about the gills,' said Snub.

'Just thoughtful,' said Rollison. 'Something to drink, Jolly.'

He went into the room and saw Judith standing by an armchair near the window.

He was struck by her pale face and troubled eyes and wondered just how much she knew about Mellor's reputation, whether he had been wrong in his first good opinion of her. She wore a black two-piece suit with a plain white blouse; it would serve as mourning. When he smiled at her she raised her hands, as if to ward off an impending blow. Immediately he was angry with himself, for he had forgotten the anxiety which she must be feeling. Snub must have told her something of the truth.

'Is he—' she began but couldn't go on.

'He'll pull through,' said Rollison.

She caught her breath. 'Are you sure?'

'I'm quite sure; I've just telephoned the

doctor.'

'Oh,' she said.

She put her hands behind her, groping for the chair, and Snub slipped quickly across the room and helped her to sit down. She leaned back, her eyes closed, and Rollison knew that she was fighting against tears. He knew more than that: she believed in Mellor and she had told the truth as she knew it. He did not doubt that again throughout the case.

'Whisky for the lady,' Snub said and came close to Rollison. 'Her nerves have been stretched as tight as a drum. You haven't just tried to cheer her up, have you?'

'No, Mellor will pull through.'

'Fine! A very lucky young man, in my opinion,' said Snub. 'How's everything?'

'Bad.' Rollison took a whisky-and-soda from the tray which Jolly held in front of him, Snub took another and carried it to the girl. 'I want you a minute,' Rollison added and went with Jolly into the kitchen.

It was small, spotless, white-tiled; the pans shone, everything was in its appointed place.

Jolly closed the door.

'I hope there has been no trouble, sir.'

'We're in a jam but we'll get out of it,' Rollison said. 'Nothing really serious. How did you get on with the police? Did they learn anything about Asham Street?'

'Not from *us*, sir.'

'Good! Were they difficult?'

'Insistent but I think they believed all that we told them.'

'They won't in future. Grice is on the warpath and there is a general feeling that Mellor is a real bad hat. What's all this about Waleski?'

Jolly said solemnly: 'It was really somewhat ridiculous, sir. The man was still in the kitchen when the police arrived and he offered no violence. He accused you of assaulting him and even preferred a charge. I made no comment, thinking you would best be able to deal with the situation. The police took the gun which was found in the flat—*his* gun, I believe. Miss Lorne told them about the man who had attacked her and also about the note which she received. There was some annoyance displayed when the note could not be found.'

Rollison laughed. 'They can have it; run it over for prints first, Jolly, and see whether we've anything in our private collection. Then ring Grice up and apologise because I absent-mindedly slipped it into my pocket.'

'Very good, sir.'

'And test this other note for prints, too.' Rollison pulled out of his pocket the letter he had picked up in Mellor's room. 'But don't let the police have that. It's Exhibit A for the private collection. Very likely you'll find no prints except Mellor's and mine. If there are any others, they'll probably be the same on each.'

'I'll see to it,' promised Jolly.

'Thanks.'

'I hope the situation isn't really grave,' said Jolly earnestly. 'It has already become a very different affair from what we first anticipated. I suppose—' Jolly paused, as if diffident, but actually to give greater emphasis to what he had to say and Rollison eyed him expectantly. 'I suppose there is no doubt at all, sir, that James Mellor is Sir Frederick Arden's son? Because if you are wrong in that assumption then it would greatly alter the complexion of the case, wouldn't it?'

'No.'

'I beg your pardon,' said Jolly, startled.

'The complexion of the case is the same— Judith Lorne having a rough time, funny business in one of the East End gangs and a warning-off both by Grice and Bill Ebbutt. If you mean it's no longer a gentle inquiry to soothe Sir Frederick Arden's feelings, you're right; but that changed when we knew Mellor was wanted for Galloway's murder, didn't it?'

'I suppose it did,' conceded Jolly. 'May I say I hope you won't take too many chances, sir.'

'We'll have a chat about it later,' said Rollison. 'I want to hide Mellor. Ebbutt won't help and he can't come here. Any idea?'

Jolly said: 'That makes it very difficult.'

'Meaning, no ideas,' Rollison smiled. 'All right, Jolly, I think I know where we can park him. There are a few don'ts for the list. Don't let the police know that I'm doing anything for Sir Frederick Arden. Tell Miss Lorne not to mention the name Arden to them. They won't necessarily tie it up with Sir Frederick. Don't say anything to the Press if anyone comes or rings up; don't let her leave the flat and don't leave it yourself until I get back.'

'Very good, sir. Are there any positive instructions?'

Rollison chuckled. 'You do me more good than a bottle of champagne! Yes. Tell Snub that I want him to go East and find out whether there's any talk in Asham Street, whether the police have discovered there was funny business at Number 51. He's to report immediately if the police have got that far. And if anyone wants me, you don't know where I am.'

'Where will you be, sir?'

'At Pulham Gate,' said Rollison; 'and I hope to come straight back here.'

*　　　*　　　*

He spent ten minutes talking to Judith and trying to reassure her. He judged that she was dangerously near a collapse: the strain of the past month had taken a heavy toll of her nervous resistance and today's shock had shaken her badly. She presented a problem in herself, the greater because he knew that she had no close relatives and was dependent entirely on her own resources. When he left for 7, Pulham Gate, where Sir Frederick Arden lived, he was in a pessimistic mood; there was so much he didn't know and couldn't see.

At least the police didn't follow him.

*   *   *

Dusk was falling when he reached Kensington, the lamps in the wide thoroughfare of Pulham Gate were lit and over this district of large, pale-grey houses and private squares there was the hush of evening. Lights showed at some of the tall windows and Rollison switched on the sidelights of the Rolls-Bentley before he left the car. He looked up and down, almost by habit, and the only person near by was a policeman. He saw the man coming towards him and was puzzled without knowing why. He turned to the steps leading to the front door of Number 7 and the policeman called out:

'Excuse me, sir.' He had a reedy voice.

'Hallo?'

'Aren't you Mr Richard Rollison? The *Hon*ourable Richard Rollison?'

'Yes.'

'I thought so,' said the policeman in a tone of great satisfaction. 'I'm afraid I must ask you to come along with me, sir. I hope you won't

94

give any trouble.'

'So do I,' said Rollison. The reedy voice and the puzzling fact which he couldn't quite place took on a greater significance. 'What's all this about?'

'They'll tell you at the station.'

'Which station?'

'Now don't be awkward,' said the constable; 'it won't do you no good.' He glanced past Rollison who heard a car coming towards him. 'Here's the squad car, there's a call out for you. Don't be awkward,' he repeated.

He now sounded almost pleading—and the warning note rang loudly in Rollison's mind.

The car pulled up.

Rollison glanced at it. There were two men inside and they made no attempt to get out. They were small men and the warning became a clarion call. These were not policemen.

The man in uniform gripped his arm.

'Here we are, so don't give us no trouble. It will only be the worse for you if you do.'

'So this is a pinch,' said Rollison, mildly.

'That's it,' said the constable. He pulled Rollison towards the car—a pre-war Morris of a kind which the police had used for the Flying Squad but had turned in years ago—and opened the door. One of the men—the man next to the driver—looked round. 'Inside, please.'

Rollison lowered his head, started to get in—and then moved his left arm and tipped the heads of the two men forward. Their hats fell off and he gripped their heads and cracked them together. The crack resounded; one man gasped and the other made a curious grunting sound. Rollison back-heeled, catching the constable on the shin and, as the man let him go, he darted back and straightened up. The policeman was swaying on one leg and putting his right hand into his pocket at the same time; there was an evil glint in his eyes. Rollison swung a left to his chin, jolting his arm when the blow connected.

He heard nothing of the next approaching car until brakes squealed. He glanced round to see a gleaming American model, sleek and streamlined back and front, pulling in behind the Morris. A woman was at the wheel—a lovely creature. The thing which most surprised him was her composure: she showed no sign of alarm.

'Stay there!' he called. 'Stay where you are!'

She opened the door of the car and swung slim, nylon-sheathed legs on to the pavement. The policeman had recovered but he made no further attack, simply rushed to the Morris. The engine was turning over, the men inside had recovered from the collision. As the constable bent down to get inside, the car began to move.

'Aren't you going to stop them?' asked the woman.

She was tall. As she reached Rollison he was

aware of a delicate perfume, of a pair of gleaming, beautiful blue eyes—yes, a lovely creature. His hand throbbed and he was short of breath.

'No,' he said, shortly.

'The police—' she began, only to break off.

'Wasn't he a policeman?' Rollison asked.

'What *is* all this?' she demanded.

'Rehearsals for a fancy-dress ball,' said Rollison. 'It's being photographed—the camera is on the roof.'

She glanced upwards while the Morris swung round a corner, engine roaring.

There was a sharp edge to the woman's voice when she spoke next.

'Are you playing the fool?'

'Yes. In fact this was a hold-up. Thank you for coming in the nick of time.' He smiled more freely and there was laughter in his tone. 'Haven't we met before?'

She drew back.

'I don't think so,' she said but suddenly her expression changed; she came nearer, as if trying to study his face more clearly. 'Are you—Mr *Rol*lison?'

'Yes.'

'Oh. Has this anything to do with'—she looked at Number 7—'the work you are doing for my uncle.'

'I doubt it. I always try to do too many things at once and sometimes they overlap.'

He had placed her as Arden's niece, of

whom he had heard but whom he had met only once, and that some time ago at a Charity Ball. He knew her by reputation as a leader of the Smart Set which had defied austerity; as one of the beauties of the day and a woman of keen intelligence and incomparable selfishness. He hadn't realised that she knew he was working for Arden but didn't think much about that then. As he waited for her to speak again, he was thinking about the welcome he'd received, the speed of the attempt to kidnap him and all the implications.

But she gave him little time to think.

'Aren't you going to send for the police?'

'No one's hurt,' he said, 'and I probably asked for it.'

They eyed each other for some seconds and a youth passed, staring at them as he went by. It was darker now. The dusk filmed her face and gave it an ethereal glow. She was perfectly dressed, her poise and carriage were delightful—and he felt that her reputation for keen intelligence was not falsely founded.

'If I hear aright, one day you will probably ask for more than you want to get,' she said dryly. 'Were you going to see my uncle or coming away?'

'Going.'

'When I left this afternoon he was very poorly. I'm not sure that you ought to see him. The doctors have warned him against excitement and you always seem to excite him.'

'I'm sorry,' he said. 'It's my baneful influence.'

'This is not funny. He is a very sick man.'

'Yes,' said Rollison. 'Yes.' They still faced each other and he was reminded of the challenge which he had seen in Waleski's eyes. 'I think he'll pull through, though, with luck and a fair deal.'

'Must you talk in riddles?'

'Which was the riddle?' asked Rollison.

She looked away from him.

'I think we should go indoors: we can't talk here, Mr Rollison.'

She led the way and he followed thoughtfully, wondering whether he had touched her on a sore spot when he had talked of luck and a square deal for Sir Frederick Arden. Perhaps she expected to inherit a substantial sum on the old man's death; and she might be anxious to remove the next-of-kin. He had not been able to see her during the case until now because she had been in Paris; he did not think she had been expected back so soon. He wished she hadn't arrived at this moment, he had needed more time to recover from the sudden assault from the phoney policeman.

She opened the front door with a key.

He followed her into the house, thinking again about the assault. The phoney policeman and his companions had known that he was likely to come here, had chosen this spot for their ambush because he wouldn't expect trouble there; a neat trick. He knew now why the uniformed man had puzzled him: the real plodding gait of a policeman had been missing. The policeman had been armed. As he hadn't fired, he had obviously come to kidnap, not to kill. The only reason anyone interested in this affair could want to kidnap him was to make him talk. It was safe to say that he had 'them' worried, that this was the second false move he had forced in twelve hours, but there was a serious doubt at the back of his mind.

Had they sped away without shooting because they wanted him alive, not dead? Or had the woman's arrival driven them off?

CHAPTER NINE

The Millionaire

The spacious hall was dimly lighted, great bear-skin rugs were spread over the polished parquet floor, two landscapes in oils hung on the high walls, their beauty half-hidden in the poor light. The curving staircase was on the right, a circular lounge-hall beyond the entrance hall was beautifully furnished. About this house was an air of comfort, luxury and good taste.

A footman appeared and bowed.

'Good evening, Miss Clarissa.'

'William, find out whether Sir Frederick is resting and come and let me know.'

She turned into the drawing-room as the footman bowed again; he only glanced at Rollison. Rollison followed her into a wide, spacious room where two great glass chandeliers glistened and sparkled, although the only light came from wall-lamps. In a far corner a grand piano stood in red-tinged dignity. The colour scheme here was dark red and grey.

Clarissa Arden tugged the rope of a bell.

'I want to know why you don't wish to send for the police,' she said; her voice was cold enough to sound haughty.

'That's simple. They would want to know what I was doing here. That would involve your uncle. I think some kinds of excitement would be bad for him.'

She stood, tall and imposing, with her back to a fine Adam fireplace, weighing her words. Before she spoke she glanced towards the door as if to make sure that it was shut. Then she said clearly:

'I don't think I like you, Mr Rollison.'

'I hope that won't stop you from offering me a drink,' he said and smiled at her.

The two encounters had stimulated him,

101

lifting the blanket of depression which had dropped after the talk with Grice and Ebbutt.

The door opened and an elderly butler said: 'You rang, Miss Clarissa?'

'Whisky?' she asked Rollison.

'Please.'

'Bring whisky, Samuel, and gin,' said Clarissa Arden. When the door closed behind the butler she went on: 'I'm not at all sure that you are a good influence on my uncle. I am told that usually after your visits he suffers a relapse. He is not well enough to know what is good for him just now. I think I must ask you not to come again, Mr Rollison.'

'Ah. Did you take medical and legal advice?'

She frowned. 'This is no time for facetiousness.'

'That wasn't facetious; I'm in earnest. Doctors can say and lawyers decide whether a man is in his right mind or whether he isn't. If your uncle isn't, I might be persuaded to stay away. If he is, I'd like him to be judge of whether I come or not.'

She said: 'How does it feel to be so clever?'

'Between ourselves, it's a pain in the neck; but we have to learn to bear our burdens, don't we?'

He offered cigarettes and she took one. As he lit it for her he looked into her eyes and saw the secret smile in them. It remained when she drew her head back and let smoke trickle from her nostrils; he wished she hadn't done that because it spoiled perfection. She was nearly as tall as he and, standing like that with her head back and looking at him through her lashes, there was a touch of mystery about her; and mockery?

'Who attacked you outside?' she asked.

'Mr Waleski's comrades,' said Rollison promptly.

He'd been waiting for the chance to speak of Waleski and, although the words came casually, he was alert for any change in her expression. There were two: a quick flash of surprise, almost of alarm; a quicker flash of self-warning when she told herself that she must give nothing away. Then the mask dropped again. He thought of her as being covered by a veil, filmy and hardly noticeable.

She wasn't quite real.

'Whom did you say?'

'I thought you might know Comrade Waleski,' said Rollison sadly. 'He and I had a chat this afternoon and I've been told that what he wishes for me is a painful death or a few nights in the lock-up. But he's really of no account.'

He glanced towards a miniature by the fireplace but watched her closely. Again he saw her quick flash of interest before the veil dropped again.

She overplayed her hand when she said:

'If he's of no account, you needn't worry about him.'

'I don't,' said Rollison.

She started to speak but Samuel came in—a stately man with exactly the right manner; a rival to Jolly.

'That's all, Samuel,' said Clarissa Arden.

'Very good, miss.'

The butler put the tray on a small table and Rollison went towards it, picking up the gin. There was a large array of bottles: Italian and French vermouth, fruit squashes, whisky, a syphon and a small jug of water, some bitters—everything they might need.

'What will you have with the gin?' asked Rollison. 'Oh—may I mix it?'

'Dry vermouth,' she said. 'What made you think I might know this Waleski?'

Rollison busied himself with the bottles and glasses.

'Intuition. Didn't you know about my intuition? It is one of the burdens I have to carry. In vulgar parlance, we say hunches. You know, Miss Arden, you don't keep abreast of the popular Press. Almost any national newspaper will tell you, sooner or later, that I work by hunches and have a genius for stumbling upon the truth. It's all done by accident, of course—no praise even where praise is due. I fix a man or woman with my eagle eye, as you'll see in a minute, and read the truth behind their inscrutable expression.'

'How marvellous!' she said dryly.

'I've been at it for so long I ought to be

good,' said Rollison blandly. He handed her the gin-and-vermouth, smiled almost inanely, looking for a moment as if he meant every word he said. 'Here's a long life to your uncle!'

He sipped—and as she put the glass to her lips, his expression changed. The bleakness was there; and something more: a cool, cold appraisal, by which he told her that her beauty, her intelligence, her composure, had made no impression on him. It also told her that he believed she knew much more than she had yet admitted and that from now on she would have to deal with him.

She held the glass steady but didn't drink.

Rollison murmured: 'Not a toast you approve?'

She drank quickly and put her glass down. She seemed shaken, as if that sudden transformation had alarmed her. There was also speculation in her gaze. Which was the real man: the one she had glimpsed or the amiable fop who now smiled fatuously at her and said:

'What should we do without Scotch?'

The door opened and the footman came in.

'Well, William?' Clarissa's voice was husky.

'Sir Frederick is awake, Miss, and would like to see Mr Rollison.'

'Will you tell him to say I'll be up in a few minutes?' Rollison asked.

The woman hesitated; then nodded.

The footman went out. Rollison sipped his drink again then stubbed his cigarette in a heavy glass ash-tray. As he did so, he said:

'You won't be wise to upset your uncle and it will upset him if you try to keep me away.'

'I don't think you are half as good as you think you are, Mr Rollison.'

'Even that would be pretty good, wouldn't it?' murmured Rollison. 'Shall I see you again before I go?'

She didn't answer. He finished his drink and went out. William was at the foot of the stairs and turned and led the way up. The hush about the house seemed to become more intense here, perhaps because the thick carpet on the stairs and landing muffled every sound of their footsteps. William, tall, slender and good-looking, led the way along a wide passage to Arden's rooms. It was a suite: study, dressing-room, bedroom and bathroom; no other rooms were near it.

Arden sat in his study, wearing a beige-coloured dressing-gown, his thin grey hair standing on end, thick-lensed glasses making his eyes look large. He hadn't shaved for two or three days and passed his hand over the grey bristles; a nervous habit. His feet were pushed into carpet slippers and he sat in a large hide armchair, his feet close to the fireplace where a small coal-fire burned. The heavy brown curtains were drawn and the room was very warm.

'Ah, Rollison. Where have you been?' Arden's voice was gruff and he slurred the words—that slurring had started when he had recovered from the seizure which had nearly killed him. 'Expected you all day.'

'I've been busy,' Rollison said.

'My affairs.'

'Yes.'

'All right, all right, come and sit down.'

Arden motioned to a smaller armchair opposite him. His hands were long and thin, the blue veins stood out, the backs were covered with purply brown freckles. Everything about him was long and thin: face, nose, body, hands and feet. Standing, he was six feet five and at seventy-one showed no sign of a stoop.

The study was friendly: a comfortable man's room with book-lined walls, an old, carved oak desk on which were two photographs, of a young man and a middle-aged woman. They were the dead son and the dead wife.

He held his hands towards the fire; they had a transparent look.

'Have you found him?'

'I shall,' Rollison said.

'You've said that all along. I'm beginning to doubt if you'll ever succeed. I thought I could rely on you but I'm not happy, Rollison. Not at all happy. Are you sure you're doing everything you can?'

'Yes. Too much. I shouldn't have told you

his name.'

Arden said slowly:

'I would have known, Rollison. I had a telephone message—telling me Mellor was my son. Someone already knew. Rollison, I'm frightened, sometimes, by the hatred behind all this. I—Never mind! Don't want to be rude. I know you're trying but I'm tormented by thoughts of that boy. If I had—' he broke off and grumbled under his breath. 'Never mind. It's ridiculous nonsense to suggest he might have killed anyone. Don't forget that you're to find out who did commit the murder. It won't be enough just to find my son.'

Rollison wondered what Sir Frederick would do if he knew what Grice and Ebbutt thought of Mellor.

'Why don't you say something? Eh? Look here, Rollison!' The seizure and the constant illness had not dimmed the grey eyes or taken away their fire or affected the alertness of the keen mind. 'You're keeping something back. What is it? What have you done to your hand? Been fighting?'

'Yes.'

'Who?'

'The enemies of your son.'

'Ah!' Arden drew back his hands and clenched them tightly; like claws. 'So you've discovered something? You know his enemies. Who are they? Rollison, I want the truth! I don't want to hear any of that nonsense about keeping bad news away from me. I can stand a shock. What do the fools think I am? A stone image? I want to *know*, Rollison. What have you found?'

Rollison said slowly: 'Your son.'

Arden didn't speak. His hands tightened upon each other, he peered intently into Rollison's face and his frail body was rigid. Rollison could hear his breath rattling up and down his wind-pipe. He lost a little colour— and then suddenly his hands unclenched and he ran one over his chin.

'Is that true?'

'Yes.'

'Is he all right?'

'He'll live.'

'So—he is ill?' The words were like a sigh.

'He's been ill,' Rollison said. 'He's in good hands now and I'm assured that he'll be as good as new in a few days.'

'I want to see him.'

'No,' said Rollison. 'That wouldn't do just yet.'

'Nonsense! I'm going to see him.'

'I thought you wanted to help him.'

'Don't bandy words. What harm will it do if I see him?'

'It's too early. If you're going to trust me, you'll have to trust me all the way.' Rollison took out his cigarette-case, put a cigarette to his lips and flicked his lighter. The flame burned steadily until he remembered that tobacco-smoke upset the old man; was liable to start a paroxysm of coughing which might bring on another heart attack. He put the lighter out. 'I'm not the only one seeking your son, you know; but the others haven't found him yet.'

Arden grunted: 'Police?'

'Yes.'

'*Hmm*. Can you keep him away from the police?'

'I think so. It's one of the things I want to talk to you about. If they find him, they'll charge him with Galloway's murder right away. At the moment he's in hiding in the East End of London but he can't stay there for long. I want to move him somewhere safe where he'll get good attention and be free from prying eyes, from his own enemies and from the police. I don't know of such a place offhand. Do you?'

Arden barked: 'Bring him here!'

'No, that won't do.'

'Why won't it?'

'You know why. I don't trust your household.'

'I'm not sure you're right about that,' growled Arden, 'but I've been better since you told me what to do. I sent that advertisement to *The Times* for a footman at the Lodge. Something's gone amiss; it's actually in today.' He sniffed. 'My improvement since I've measured out my own medicine, as you

110

suggested, might be a coincidence, might be—' He broke off, his voice became querulous. 'Expense doesn't matter, I've told you that often enough. Can't you find a comfortable place where they'll look after him and ask no questions?'

'I could if he weren't wanted for murder.'

'The *fools*!' Arden ran his hand over his chin again. 'The damned fools! *Murder!* My son! Where do you want him to be? In London?'

'Not too far away but not in London proper.'

'He'll have to go to the Lodge. You can trust the servants for that.'

'I don't trust your servants anywhere.' He had to be emphatic about that, lest the old man relaxed the precautions he had already taken. 'I want a small place—a cottage would do—with someone who'll do what you tell them and hold their peace. When I suggested that you should go away, you mentioned an old woman who lives near Woking—your ex-housekeeper. Would she do this?'

Arden said slowly, yet eagerly: 'Why, yes, *ye-es*! Why didn't I think of Mrs Begbie? Yes, she'll look after him.' He started to get up. 'I'll give you a note to her, you're to tell her that nothing will be too good for him. When will you take him? Tonight?'

'Just as soon as I can,' promised Rollison. 'You've got to understand one thing, Arden.'

'Yes, yes. What is it?'

'The police might find him and that would

111

make me powerless—except to look for the real murderer. I can promise nothing but there's an even chance that I can get him safely to this cottage.'

'I'll have to rely on you,' said Arden. 'If I were ten years younger—Never mind, never mind! I like you, Rollison, trust you. God help me if I'm wrong.'

He stood up to his full height, reached the desk and sat down slowly in a swivel chair. He wrote slowly but in a clear, bold hand. But it was not at the long, thin fingers or the pen held so steadily that Rollison stared; it was at the pale blue note-paper.

CHAPTER TEN

Paper And Ink

Arden gave his full attention to writing the note. Rollison looked away, telling himself that the paper being the same colour as that of the crumpled note which he'd found in Mellor's room and left with Jolly to test for prints was sheer coincidence. He reached forward, took a sheet of the note-paper from the desk and scribbled on it, as if making a reminder note. He folded it carefully and slipped it into his wallet. The old man's pen scratched with its slow, regular movements and the wheezing breath rumbled and rattled loudly. A coal fell into the fender but did not disturb Arden's concentration.

Rollison glanced about the room. His gaze reached the door, passed it, went back again.

The door was open; and he knew that he had closed it. He stood up, still without distracting Arden's attention, and mechanically put a cigarette to his lips. He remembered not to light it as he crossed the room silently.

Yes, the door was open—very little: no more than half an inch. But anyone outside could hear anything that was being said inside. When had it been opened? His back had been towards it and he'd heard nothing. Whoever was there might have heard about the cottage and Mrs Begbie.

'Was' there? Or had been?

He opened the door quickly but without a sound—and Clarissa Arden started back, stifling an exclamation.

Arden looked up.

'What's that?'

'It's warm in here,' said Rollison without looking round. The woman backed a pace and stared at him. In the half-light of the landing she looked unreal, a figure of ghostly beauty.

'I like it warm. I've finished. She'll—'

'Everything will be all right,' Rollison interrupted and closed the door as Clarissa turned and walked quickly away. He crossed

113

to Arden who was slipping the note into a pale blue envelope. 'That's nice note-paper,' he remarked.

Arden grunted. 'Never mind the note-paper. See that Mrs Begbie gets that herself before the boy arrives. Understand me, don't you? She lives alone. No difficulty—reliable woman. Or I always thought she was reliable, always thought all my servants were.'

'We'll make sure,' said Rollison.

'Damn the servants! Look after my son.' Arden stood up and peered down on Rollison. There was something pathetic in his gaze, in the way he stretched out a hand and rested it on Rollison's shoulder. 'I know you think I'm a foolish old man. Perhaps I am. But life catches up with you, Rollison. Remember that while you're still young. Do something wrong, let it fade out of memory for a while, and you'll think that it's dead, buried, forgotten; but it isn't. It's always there, always ready to haunt you, as this is haunting me. Commit a wrong—and put it right as soon as you can. Do you understand?'

'I know.'

'Yes,' said Arden. 'Yes, I really believe you do. Remarkable man, Rollison! I'm glad I asked you to help me. I—Oh, forget it; doesn't matter. I was going to say something else before I started preaching. What on earth— Oh, yes. Come and sit down—'

'I ought to go.'

'Come and sit down!' Arden went slowly to his chair. Rollison did likewise. 'Now listen to me. I sent a cheque for ten thousand pounds to my solicitors today. Kemble, Wright and Kemble, Lincoln's Inn. They are to cash it at once, place it in a separate account and use it on your instructions if I die before it's wanted.'

Rollison said slowly: 'Why did you do that?'

The man's voice and his manner were impressive; this was of real importance to him.

'I don't think I shall live long,' Arden said abruptly. 'I shouldn't be surprised if—Hmm, never mind. The money is to be used for my son's defence, just for his defence, understand me? That's if I die before this business is over and he's not cleared of suspicion. You won't take any money now, so—well, there it is. Don't spare any expense, Rollison, and understand that you can use the money for any purpose you like provided it helps the boy.'

'We'll finish the job while you're still able to enjoy life,' said Rollison.

'I don't know—I really don't know. It's a safeguard, anyhow. I confess there's nothing I'd like more than to see him clear of this trouble, happy and settled—nothing! I've a dream, Rollison—a silly old man's dream. I'd like to see the boy married to a good woman before I die. A good woman, like my wife.'

He broke off and gazed dreamily into space.

Rollison murmured: 'Your niece?'

The old man started.

'Eh? Clarissa?' he laughed and began to cough, pressed his hand against his chest and breathed wheezily, with great difficulty. Then he regained his breath and his smile twisted his whole face. 'I wouldn't wish any man to marry Clarissa. She's an empty shell, Rollison. Beautiful, I grant you, but—made of ice. She's sacrificed her life wantonly to the pursuit of excitement. Mixing my metaphors aren't I? If she weren't so well off, I'd say—Never mind, never mind; forget it.'

'Is she wealthy?'

'Her father was; she inherited everything of his only a few years ago. Oh, she's no motive for wanting me dead!' He laughed again and this time managed without a spasm of coughing. 'Even if she were as poor as a church mouse, she'd still have no motive for wanting me dead, although she may think she has. She hasn't seen my will. She's just back from Paris. Said she'd heard I was ill and wanted to come and look after me. She meant she was tired of her latest lover. London's her happy hunting-ground. But never mind Clarissa—except don't trust her. She'll try to get her claws into you because you're an unusual man—something different. She'd stand by and watch me die if it would give her a thrill. Forget her! Why are you sitting there, wasting your time? I thought you had a lot to do.'

116

The passage was empty.

Rollison walked to the landing and looked along another passage which was at right angles to the first. Three rooms led from it and all the doors were closed. The first was unlocked; it led to a large bedroom which obviously wasn't in use. The next door was locked. He hesitated outside the third, then tried the handle; the door opened and light showed. He pushed the door a little wider so that he could see into the room. No one spoke so he slipped inside.

It was a large bedroom, beautifully furnished, with a modern silvered oak suite; obviously a woman's room. On an oval table near the window a bowl of red tulips reminded him of the flowers in the window of 49, Asham Street. The high double bed was spread with gleaming satin, the pale grey carpet had a deep pile; this was a room of luxury. The dressing-table had three long mirrors; a wardrobe occupied most of one wall. There was a faint smell of perfume which he recognised as Clarissa's.

He closed the door.

Someone moved in another room which led from a corner of this; he could see enough to tell him that it was a bathroom.

Clarissa didn't come out of there.

117

He went to the writing-desk, near the tulips; pale blue note-paper and envelopes were in the rack. There were sheets die-stamped *7, Pulham Gate, SW8*, others which were quite plain—the size of the paper on which the note to Mellor had been written. He took one of the plain sheets and slipped it into his pocket. The small waste-paper basket was half-full of crumpled paper and used envelopes. He picked it up, found three envelopes addressed to Clarissa Arden at this address, put them into his pocket and replaced the waste-paper basket. As he straightened up, she came out of the bathroom.

She caught her breath at sight of him.

'Oh, hallo,' said Rollison brightly. 'I thought I'd return the call.'

'Leave this room at once!'

'Haughty is as haughty does,' murmured Rollison. 'I think we've a lot to say to each other, precious. It's naughty and unhealthy to eavesdrop. I don't think you quite understand the situation or that I can get tough.'

'I told you to leave this room.'

'All in good time. In spite of your false testimony your uncle has been showing signs of improved health. If he stops improving I shall regard your homecoming as more than a coincidence. You're very lovely, Clarissa—too lovely to have your neck stretched by a hempen rope. But they do hang women and even your money and position wouldn't save you from a trial. Remember that, every time you get thoughtless and every time you prowl, won't you?'

'If you don't leave at once I shall tell Samuel to send for the police.'

'Well, well!' breathed Rollison. 'What a lot you have in common with Comrade Waleski!' She flinched and he went towards her, even took her hands, as if they were old, tried friends. 'Clarissa, don't mix with bad men. There may be a spice of excitement, and you may like the breath of danger, but these are really bad men and I should hate to think you were really a bad woman.'

She took her hands away and slapped his face.

'That must be the touch of the Brontës in you,' murmured Rollison. 'One final word. When in need, come and see me. I love listening to damsels in distress.'

Her cheeks were white and her lips quivering, her eyes stormy. He smiled and turned away, crossed the room unhurriedly and looked back at her from the door. His eyes were laughing; hers were still furious.

The ice that was in Clarissa Arden had melted.

Snub hadn't returned when Rollison reached Gresham Terrace. Jolly, who opened the door, raised a hand to exhort silence and whispered that Miss Lorne was sleeping on the sofa in the living-room. Rollison looked in. She was

119

fast asleep, a silken cushion beneath her head, a travelling-rug thrown over her.

'You make a good nurse,' murmured Rollison. 'How are you amusing yourself?'

'I've been testing the note-paper,' said Jolly. 'There are some prints which I can't identify and which don't appear to be Mellor's or Miss Lorne's. Will you come and see, sir?'

Once Jolly's room had been large—nearly as large as Rollison's. A few months ago, however, Jolly had suggested that a partition be erected so that he could have both a bedroom and a 'den.' The 'den' was approached by a low door in the wooden partition. Beyond was Jolly's idea of heaven. He was an enthusiastic amateur photographer with a talent which had only lately been developed; most of the work he did for Rollison, on such affairs as this. He had also worked diligently on the simpler scientific side of criminal investigation and had equipment here which had once been mildly approved by Grice. On a bench beneath the window was a microscope, a bunsen burner, a number of elementary chemical solutions and in the drawers and cupboards which made the den seem tiny was all the paraphernalia of detection including equipment for taking finger-prints. On top of one case were Jolly's text-books: Gross's *Criminal Investigation*, Glaiser's *Medical Jurisprudence and Toxicology* and works of lesser renown but equal merit

120

and usefulness.

Rollison seldom ventured here; never without an invitation.

Some photographs of finger-prints were pinned to a small wooden board and by them was a magnifying-glass.

'These need enlarging but you can see them clearly through the glass,' said Jolly.

'Yes. Run powder over these, will you?'

Rollison gave him the envelopes addressed to Clarissa Arden and Jolly opened a small bottle containing grey powder over the envelopes. Prints showed up almost immediately. He blew the powder away gently. As the prints became clearer, he glanced swiftly at Rollison and his voice quivered slightly with excitement.

'I think you've made a discovery of importance, sir.'

Rollison said: 'Same prints?'

'I'm almost sure. Will you kindly use the glass?'

The prints were huge behind the lens. There were several different ones on each envelope but most were badly smudged, whereas some prints were sharp, clear and superimposed on the others. These were probably the prints which Clarissa had made when she had opened the letters. The loops and whorls had characteristics which could not be confused with the broader prints of the people who had first handled the envelopes.

Rollison turned to the note which read: *The best way to disappear is to die.* Identical prints were there, much fainter, and with other prints superimposed which he guessed were Mellor's.

Jolly breathed: 'Am I right, sir?'

'I think you are,' said Rollison slowly. 'Miss Arden handled the note-paper before Mellor received it.'

'So *she* sent it.'

'Let's stick to what we know; she handled the paper.'

'And no one else did, sir, except Mellor and you. Your prints show at two of the corners where you held the paper cautiously. Mellor's are very clear, top right and centre both sides—where you would expect them to be when he took the note out. Hers are on both sides and fairly general, the kind of prints that one would make when writing a letter and folding it for an envelope. Have you met Miss Arden?'

Rollison laughed. 'Yes, and we're not friends. Like some fresh air, Jolly?'

'Exactly as you wish, sir. I have prepared a supper tray.'

'Good. Go to the Oxford Palace Hotel and find out what you can about Waleski. The police may be watching to see if inquiries are made for him but cock a snook at any policemen. I'm anxious to know whether Clarissa Arden has called on Waleski. I'll wait

122

here until you return or telephone.'

*   *   *

Rollison sat in an armchair, near the desk and the telephone. The wall behind the desk was filled with a remarkable miscellany of souvenirs of criminal cases: weapons used for murder; poisons; odd trophies of the hunt. The star piece was a hempen noose; it was Rollison's boast that a particularly savage murderer had been hanged with it. This was called the Trophy Wall.

Judith still slept, breathing evenly, looking calm and delightful without any sign of strain—as if she were really resting for the first time for weeks. Jolly could exert a remarkably soothing effect and had doubtless impressed her with his view of Rollison's omnipotence. Now and again she stirred but didn't wake. Rollison watched her as he thought of Arden, Clarissa, everyone whom he had seen that day. He was trying to put every incident in its proper perspective, to judge the importance of one against the other; and, finally, to judge when it would be necessary and wise to go to the police. The evidence that attempts had been made on Arden's life was so slender that he doubted whether the police would pay it much attention. There was no evidence that Arden's legitimate son had been murdered. The police would say, and rightly

123

because of the facts before them, that Rollison was reading crime into a series of unrelated but coincidental circumstances.

One question mattered above all. If Mellor were arrested and charged, what would be the effect on Sir Frederick Arden? He believed that the tension and anxiety of the trial would kill the old man. That was the strongest single justification for trying to keep Mellor away from the police, for backing his own judgment.

Yes, he would have to do that if he could.

He saw Judith stir again and then the telephone bell gave a slight ring, the preliminary to steady ringing. He took the receiver off quickly before it had time to disturb the girl.

'Rollison speaking.'

'Hallo, Boss!' It was Snub who sounded bright and presumably had good news. 'Still in the land of the live and kicking.'

'How did you get on?'

'What a stickler you are for business! All right. The police haven't heard of the Asham Street incident yet and the Doc hasn't been worried. Mellor's out of danger from the carbon monoxide. I don't think there's much need for me to haunt this part of the great metropolis tonight.'

'You needn't. But I want you to hire a shooting-brake or any kind of vehicle which will take a stretcher and garage it somewhere handy to the Doc's place in the morning, very

124

likely for use before daylight.'

'I'll be ready at the crack.'

'Thanks,' said Rollison. 'Keep a look-out for the police. I don't want them to know what you've been up to. If they discover you're going to drive a van or what-not, they might tumble to the truth. If your flat is watched, go to a hotel and let me know the telephone number.'

'Oke.'

'Off you go,' said Rollison.

'Oi, have a heart! How's sweet Judy?'

'Sleeping,' said Rollison and glanced at the girl.

Her eyes, heavy with sleep, were wide open as she stared at him. He smiled at her, said good-bye to Snub and replaced the receiver. She gave an answering smile and eased herself upon the cushion. Her hair was unruly and absently she poked her fingers through it. There were red marks on her cheek where she had been lying on the creased cushion cover.

'Hungry?' asked Rollison.

She was startled. 'Well, yes, I am.' She laughed, as if that astonished her.

'Good sign,' said Rollison. 'I'll be back in a moment.'

The sandwiches were under a silver cover, on a tray; the coffee was bubbling gently in the percolator. Rollison took the tray in and, as he pushed the door open with his elbow, saw Judith standing in front of the trophy wall.

Most of his visitors were fascinated by the collection of 'exhibits'—the weapons and the souvenirs of old crimes and many modest triumphs. But Judith was paying no attention to the macabre contents of the wall: she was looking into a tiny mirror and powdering her nose.

'A *very* good sign,' said Rollison.

She turned. 'What—Oh! I feel such a wreck.'

'Jim's out of danger,' said Rollison.

Her whole face became radiant. She didn't say: 'Are you sure?' but closed her eyes for a moment and shook her head, as if she were driving an ugly vision away. Then she looked at him smiling, composed, happy.

'Thank heaven for that! Can I see him?'

'Not yet. You may or may not realise it, young woman, but the mirror you've been dolling yourself up in has a famous history. It belonged to a beauty who murdered three husbands with arsenic. The police couldn't prove she'd ever possessed any arsenic and the mirror betrayed her—some was found along the leather edge. Now perhaps you'll show a proper respect for that wall.'

Judith laughed. 'I thought it seemed a bit grim. Mr Rollison, what are Jim's chances of being acquitted?'

'Good, if we can stall long enough.'

'You're not pretending?'

'It's the simple truth. Eat your supper.'

When she began to eat the sandwiches

126

hungrily, he went on: 'The police have asked you nearly every question that can be asked and I want to repeat some of them. Had you ever any reason to think that Jim was in difficulties?'

She said: 'Absolutely none.'

'How often did you see him?'

'Practically every day. Once or twice he had to go away on business but he was never away for more than two nights. He's the manager of a small firm of printers, you know.'

'Yes. Did you ever go to the works?'

'Several times.'

'Had he any business worries?'

'He was only worried about one thing, as far as I know, and I think I should have known had there been anything else,' said Judith. 'The world situation sometimes got on his nerves. He had a rough time in the war and—well, you know what I mean. He thought everyone who talked of war was crazy and ought to be pole-axed. The news sometimes got him down.'

'*Was* it just the news? Are you sure?'

'I've never questioned that,' said Judith quietly. 'I don't think there's any doubt. I could usually guess when he'd been depressed; it would be a day when there was more cock-fighting among the United Nations or a flare-up somewhere in the world. I don't think it was related to his personal affairs. He always said he felt so helpless—that it wouldn't have been so bad if he could have done something about it himself.'

'I see,' said Rollison. 'Did you know his friends?'

'One or two of them. I don't think he had many.'

'Isn't he a friendly type?'

'Yes; but he spent a lot of time at business, often worked late and he was rather—well, impatient of most people. He used to call himself the Superior Being. Oh, that wasn't conceit! He would be laughing at himself because he hadn't patience with a lot of social chatter and the usual table-talk—any of the conventional things.'

'How long have you known him?'

'Six months—just six months.'

'Has he ever talked about himself and what he did before that?'

'Of course. I think I know almost as much about him as he knows about himself. He wasn't demobilised until two years after the war and he spent a year studying printing. His family are nearly all printers. But there wasn't scope for him in the family business and he wasn't satisfied with their old-fashioned methods anyhow, so he got this job outside. He's good at it, you know, he's no fool.'

'I'll grant that,' said Rollison. 'Did he know anyone from the East End of London?'

'I don't think so—not well, anyhow. Why?'

'It could matter.'

128

'Well, the works are at Wembley and of course he had business all over London, so he'd know customers in the East End. I hadn't given it much thought but I think he spent one day a week in that district—or part of a day. Bethnal Green and Whitechapel mostly, I believe. You could get all the details from the works.'

'Who's managing the works now?' asked Rollison.

'The directors. The man I saw told me that they wouldn't replace Jim yet but that was nearly a month ago when I went to see if they knew anything about him. The police hadn't questioned me then and I couldn't understand what had happened to him.'

'Do you remember the name of the man you saw there?'

'Yes,' said Judith. 'Arthur Dimond. I— What's the matter?' She looked alarmed when Rollison began to choke on a sandwich. 'Have I said anything startling?'

'You've said plenty,' said Rollison, very softly, 'and you've proved me a dumbwit, Punch! I haven't given half enough attention to the business side. *Di*mond—without an "a"?'

'Yes. I know because it's on the letter-heading of the company. Mr Dimond looked after another company and didn't spend much time at Wembley. Is it important?'

'It might be,' said Rollison. 'Have some

129

coffee.'

*   *   *

Arthur Dimond was a director of Jim Mellor's firm. Flash Dimond had been the leader of the gang Mellor was later supposed to lead. Coincidence could hardly stretch as far as that.

*   *   *

Judith said: 'No, thanks, I couldn't eat any more. They were delicious.'

She looked almost sorrowfully at the few sandwiches left on the dish.

It was a quarter of an hour since she had named Arthur Dimond and she had answered many more questions since, most of which Rollison had put absently as he thought of this new angle. He had certainly not probed deeply enough into Mellor's recent past. But the police weren't blind: they must have noticed the name Dimond on that letter-heading.

'Cigarette?'

The telephone bell rang as Rollison held out his case. He put the case in her hand and dropped a lighter by her side, then went to the telephone.

'Rollison speaking.'

'Jolly, sir,' said Jolly. 'I'm speaking from a

130

call-box near the Oxford Palace Hotel. I thought I ought to communicate with you at once.'

'Yes?'

'A woman answering Miss Arden's description has called three times to see Waleski, sir, and she's just come again. Would it be wise for me to follow her?'

'Not just wise—an act of genius,' said Rollison. 'But I'll want to take over as soon as I can get there. Let me know where she goes, especially if she's likely to stay there any length of time.'

'*Very* good, sir,' said Jolly.

*   *   *

What to do with Judith and what to advise her to do? That was the most urgent problem. Was it safe to let her return to her rooms? Reason said 'yes,' instinct 'no.' There was no indication of danger for her yet; but the comrades of Waleski weren't likely to give much notice of their next move. They would want to hurt him and might decide that could best be done through Judith. She wouldn't be able to stand much more.

Judith decided to wash up.

'Jolly will never forgive you,' said Rollison, 'but carry on with the good work.'

He carried the tray into the kitchen for her, told her she would find an infinite variety of make-up in the spare room, left her puzzling why he should keep cosmetics here and went back to the telephone. He dialled a Victoria number and was not kept waiting.

'Grice speaking.'

Rollison made his voice gruff.

'Sorry to worry you, sir, but that there Torf 'as bin up to 'is tricks again.'

'Who is—Oh, Rolly, you fool.' Grice was still friendly judging from his tone. 'Where's Mellor?'

'Hoodwinking everyone like fun. I'm more interested in his girl-friend. Are you having her flat watched?'

'Why?'

'Because I want to send her home. I don't think it would be good for her to stay at this den of iniquity and I'm not sure that she'll be safe alone.'

'Any reason for saying that?'

'A bump of caution but nothing logical, Bill. Waleski was watching her place and someone did nearly strangle her. Talking of the comrade—'

'We're talking about the girl. You can safely let her go home. You'll find a sergeant in Gresham Terrace and he's there to follow her. She'll be all right.'

'Thanks,' said Rollison. 'Sworn that warrant for my arrest yet?'

'No,' said Grice. 'We've decided that Waleski's been lying and there isn't a case but

132

we could change our minds. If you run riot I shall let you cool your heels at Cannon Row for a night or two. That's clear enough, isn't it?'

'As crystal. I repeat—what are you doing with Waleski?'

'Letting him go. He's a licence for the gun and says he drew it in self-defence and didn't use it.'

'Very subtle,' said Rollison. 'You, I mean, letting him go and, I trust, keeping tabs on him. You now need two men to take care of Judith Lorne and heaven help you if you let her down. And four to follow Waleski. Bill, I think it's time we put our heads together.'

'If we don't, you'll get yours broken. I didn't expect you to take much notice of me but, if you play the fool, I won't give you an inch.'

'This isn't one of my good days,' sighed Rollison. 'No one loves me, no one believes a word I say. When I know Mellor is safely out of your reach I'll come and see you.'

He rang off, without giving Grice a chance to reply, and turned to find Judith coming in; a grave-faced Judith.

'Who was that?' she asked.

'A wise old bird, my poppet. You're going home. The police are going to make sure that no one worries you, not because they think anyone will try but because they think Mellor might come to you. If they ask more questions, tell them not a word more than you

133

have already. Refer them to me for everything else. And remember'—he was serious now—'that if you do say too much it might spoil Jim's only chance.'

'I won't spoil anything,' she promised.

He went downstairs with her and spoke to the CID man on duty, putting Judy into his charge. The girl looked small and slender beside the burly detective. The sleep and food had refreshed and encouraged her and she held her head high.

Rollison went thoughtfully back to the flat and, as he reached the landing, heard the telephone ringing. He slammed the door behind him and spoke into the extension in the hall.

'Hallo.'

'It is Jolly again, sir,' said Jolly. 'This time from the hotel. Waleski has returned and both he and the woman have gone to his room—Number 607. There is every indication that they will be there for some time.'

Rollison said: 'Oh,' and then was silent for so long that Jolly prompted him with a courteous: 'Are you still there, sir?'

'Yes, Jolly. Tell me, out of the depths of your understanding of human nature, do you think there is even a remote chance that Comrade W and mademoiselle are lovebirds?'

'Most emphatically *not*, sir.'

'Then I'll pay them a visit,' said Rollison. 'You wait there.'

134

CHAPTER ELEVEN

Spoiled Lovely

The large and glittering entrance hall of the Oxford Palace Hotel seethed and bubbled with people and talk. Rollison side-stepped a mountainous woman whose fingers seemed to be made of diamonds and her voice of sandpaper; squeezed past two men who were heartily agreeing that there was a fortune in it; and spotted Jolly.

Jolly stood, an oasis of quiet dignity in the cauldron of garish glitter, between the lifts and the staircase. As Rollison approached, a loud-voiced young woman stopped in front of Jolly and asked:

'Put me right for the Grill Room, will you?'

Jolly looked at her coldly.

'I regret, miss, I am not familiar with this establishment.'

She wilted and fled.

'Bit harsh, weren't you?' asked Rollison.

'Yes, sir.' Presumably that was not the first time Jolly had been so accosted that night.

'What of Waleski?'

'I am a little concerned about him and Miss Arden,' said Jolly, unbending. 'After due consideration I decided that this was the best position to take up but there is another

135

staircase and another lift. However, these are nearest his room—Number 607, sir. Neither of them has appeared again.'

'They'd probably come this way. Is Waleski being watched by the police?'

'I have seen three plain-clothes men but I believe there are always two or three on duty in such hotels as *this*,' said Jolly, and the faint emphasis on *this* was masterly. 'I went to the sixth floor, to make sure of the position of the room, and saw no one observing Number 607.'

'Grice wouldn't let Waleski run around on his own,' Rollison said. 'The police are just being cunning. Stay here for another five minutes, in case they come down as I go up, and then join me on the sixth floor.'

Jolly bowed, as if there were no one else to see him.

A lift was waiting, nearly full. Rollison was the only passenger to alight at the sixth floor. Here all the glitter was absent. The lights were subdued, the wide yellow-walled passages were silent, the hush reminded him of Pulham Gate. He studied the room indicator board and turned right, finding Room 607 along the first passage to the left. He made a complete tour of the floor, passing three chambermaids and a breezy American GI. When he returned to the main lift and staircase, Jolly was waiting.

'All clear?'

'Neither of them passed me, sir.'

'We'll catch 'em in a huddle,' Rollison said confidently. 'You stand at the corner of the passage and give me warning if anyone comes this way.'

'Certainly, sir. My right hand will be at my mouth if anyone approaches.'

Rollison opened the skeleton-key blade of his knife as he reached Room 607. He listened but heard no sound of voices. He slipped the key into the lock, feeling a sharp twinge of excitement. His heart beat fast as he twisted and turned. The sound of metal on metal seemed loud; surely they would hear it in the room? The key caught and he turned the lock, then glanced round at Jolly. Jolly raised his right hand and pulled his lip. Rollison left the door unlocked and stepped back, as if looking at the room numbers. A chambermaid came lolloping along with a towel over her arm. Rollison turned his back on her and walked away until she went into a room. He nipped back and received all clear from Jolly; next moment he was inside Room 607.

He stood in a tiny cubicle with two other doors. One, ajar, showed the bathroom; the other was closed.

He heard no sound, even when he stood near the closed door.

This had no lock; he knew that it could be bolted from the inside. If it were bolted, all chance of catching the couple by surprise was gone. He turned the handle and pushed; it wasn't bolted. The room beyond was dark and silent.

They might have left by the other stairs or lift; or Waleski might have heard him at the door and be lying in wait. Rollison stood quite still, breathing softly, straining his ears to catch the sound of breathing but could detect none. The faint ticking of his watch sounded. He took out his small automatic, held it in his left hand and pushed the door wider open. It made no sound at all: the hush was as uncanny as it was unexpected.

Someone passed along the passage. He kept still until the footsteps faded. Then he pushed the door another few inches and groped along the wall at shoulder height, seeking the light-switch.

He didn't find it.

He bent down, pushed the door wider and crept inside. There was no light behind him, no sound, nothing to warn anyone lurking inside that he was entering. Still crouching, he listened intently for any faint sound.

No—nothing.

He put the gun away and took a slim pencil torch from his pocket, pressed the bulb against the palm of his left hand and switched it on; his hand hid the light. He held it at arm's length then took his hand away. A slim beam of light shot out, vivid in the darkness.

If Waleski were lying in wait he would have acted by now.

Yet Rollison remained uneasy.

In the faint light he saw the pile of the carpet, the bottom of the bed and a chair. The bed was behind the door; there would be a light by the side of it. He groped for the switch, found it and, gun again at the ready, pressed it down.

Clarissa was on the bed, hair and clothes disarranged, one bare leg falling over the side of the bed, the stocking from it tied tightly round her neck.

*　　　*　　　*

'She'll do,' said Rollison.

'I'd better go on for a few more minutes, sir.'

Jolly wiped his forehead then continued to give Clarissa Arden artificial respiration. They had taken turns during the past fifteen minutes and now she was breathing more normally and was out of danger. She lay on her face and Jolly knelt on the bed, a knee on either side of her, pressing his hands into her ribs slowly, rhythmically. His sparse hair fell into his eyes and his lined face glistened with sweat.

Rollison lifted the telephone on the bedside table. Jolly glanced at him but raised no query.

'Room Service, please . . . Yes, I'll hold on.' Rollison fumbled for his cigarette-case and then tried to flick his lighter with his left hand but failed. 'Hallo, Room Service? Send some

strong coffee to Room 607 at once, please—
for three. Yes, three. Quickly, please.'

He rang off and lit the cigarette.

Jolly stopped working and heaved a great
sigh.

'I think that will do, sir.'

'Yes, take a rest,' said Rollison.

He went to the bed and lifted Clarissa,
grunting with the effort, sat her in the one
armchair and then turned down the
bedclothes. Her skirt was open at the waist
and he had loosened her girdle and
unfastened her high-necked blouse. He laid
her on the bed and pulled the bedclothes over
her then stood back to study her spoiled
beauty.

Her face was blotchy and there was a scratch
on one cheek, just below and in front of the
ear. Her hair was a tangled mass, her lipstick
smeared so that she looked as if she had been
eating strawberries with a child's greed; and
all her powder had been rubbed off. He
doubted whether Clarissa Arden had ever
looked such a wreck as she did now.

'She won't forgive us easily for this, Jolly.'

Jolly started.

'Won't forgive? I should have thought—'

'If we could tidy her up so that she looked
presentable she might remember we saved her
from dying,' said Rollison and smiled faintly.
'Of course, I could be misjudging her. When
she sees those weals at her neck, she'll know

140

that it was touch and go, won't she?'

Several weals, made by the stocking, showed red and angry on the neck which was usually so white and smooth.

She turned her head but didn't regain consciousness.

'On the whole, I prefer Miss Lorne,' said Rollison.

'Miss Arden is a very handsome woman, sir,' said Jolly, dispassionately. 'Do you mind if I wash my hands?'

'Carry on.'

'I hope to finish before the coffee arrives,' said Jolly and disappeared into the bathroom.

He was still there when the waiter arrived. Rollison took the tray at the passage door, tipped the man enough to satisfy him and not enough to make himself noticeable and carried it into the bedroom. He remembered carrying the tray into Judith and smiled—and saw Clarissa's eyelids flicker.

He went out again.

'Stay where you are for a few minutes, Jolly.'

'Very good, sir.'

Her eyes were wide open when he went back and he saw the fear in them, fear which didn't disappear when she recognised him. She caught her breath and her hands clenched beneath the clothes; they made two little mounds. He thrust his hands into his pockets, put his head on one side and murmured:

'I don't like Comrade Waleski either.'

She licked her lips.

'My—my throat is sore.'

'Nylon is bad for throats,' said Rollison. He picked up the twisted stocking and held it up and her eyes glistened with horror. 'It was tied very tightly; they didn't want you to live. Was it Waleski?'

'I—I suppose it must have been.'

'Sit up and have some coffee,' Rollison said and then called out: 'Jolly! Any aspirins?'

'Yes, sir.'

Rollison took them at the door. When he turned round, Clarissa was sitting up and looking at herself in the dressing-table mirror which was opposite the bed. She put her hands to her hair and smoothed it down while Rollison poured out black coffee, put half the sugar into the one cup and made her drink it. Now and again she glanced at him; more often into the mirror.

He poured out a second cup.

'No more,' she said and made a face.

'Two cups to complete the cure. Swallow the aspirins with this. You're lucky, Clarissa.'

She didn't answer.

'Ten or fifteen minutes longer and we might have been too late. Certainly we couldn't have pulled you round ourselves; we'd have needed a doctor, perhaps the hospital, certainly the police. If you want to leave here tonight, drink up.'

She obeyed. It was obviously difficult for her

to get the coffee down and she grimaced when she had finished. He took the cup from her and offered a cigarette.

'Thanks.'

'Feeling better?'

'I shall be all right.'

'What happened?'

She said: 'Waleski turned on me.'

'I did murmur a warning about bad men, didn't I?'

She fingered her throat gingerly, felt the ridges and craned up so that she could see her neck in the mirror. She licked her lips again and coughed on the smoke.

'He—he hit me with his cigarette-case. Here.' Her fingers poked gently through the hair at the temple.

'Why?'

'I don't know.'

'Lie number one,' said Rollison.

She held her head back and looked at him through her lashes, the same trick she had used in Pulham Gate. In spite of her ruined make-up, her loveliness was apparent. Shiny, blotchy face, smeared lipstick, rumpled hair, all failed to hide it. She was composed, too; and there was a glimmer of a smile in her eyes. Her self-control was a great tribute to her will-power.

'How do you know I haven't been lying all the time?'

He said: 'I don't. But someone tried to

murder you and Waleski had the opportunity. It might have been someone else.'

'Yes. Possibly even you.'

'Ah,' murmured Rollison. 'That's a bright notion. I almost wish I hadn't taken the stocking from your neck.'

He didn't smile; and he didn't miss the mockery in her expression. She might be bad; he was half-convinced that she was; but he didn't dislike her. She had too much courage, too quick a mind.

'Well, how do I know you didn't strangle me and then pretend to save my life?' Her husky voice drawled out the words. 'The last thing I remember is Waleski hitting me. I doubt if he would like to see me dead.'

'What's put all this into your head?'

'Worried?' She pushed her fingers through her hair and drew it tightly back from her face; it increased her beauty. 'I thought you were very anxious not to send for the police or have me taken to hospital. I couldn't believe it was for my sake, so it must be for yours. After all, if I told the police everything I know, you would be suspected, wouldn't you? Or have you got the police in your pocket?'

'They keep popping out. Why not go steaming ahead and make a job of it? There's the telephone. Just murmur "police" into it and hotel detectives will come rushing up and the police will arrive in a couple of ticks. You'd be in the fashion, too; Waleski tried to convince the police I'd man-handled him.'

'Didn't you?'

'We were talking about the telephone. It's all yours.'

Rollison sauntered to the dressing-table, dragging the easy-chair with him, and sat down. He crossed his legs and lit a cigarette.

'You'd never let me touch it,' Clarissa said.

'Go ahead.'

She frowned, as if puzzled by the challenge in his eyes; then stretched out her hand for the telephone. The graceful turn of her body drew attention to her figure; it was almost voluptuous, the movement unconsciously seductive. She held the receiver close to her ear, watching him all the time.

He kept a poker-face but his heart was thumping. He wasn't sure what she would do: only sure that if she went ahead it would ruin his chances; Grice would have to hold him on such evidence. But if she were bluffing and he called her bluff, it would prove she wanted to avoid the police.

Clarissa said: 'Chelsea 12431, please . . . thank you.'

She put the receiver down.

Rollison didn't speak. Clarissa relaxed on the pillows. There was a sound in the bathroom: Jolly, moving about uneasily. The next sound jarred through the quiet; the ringing of the telephone-bell. She took off the receiver and said:

'Can I speak to Mr Waleski?'

Rollison started; for her voice changed completely. She spoke like an American and had he not been there he would have been sure the speaker came from a Southern State. She looked at him steadily while she held on, until he heard a man's voice faintly.

Clarissa said in the same husky, attractive voice:

'Why, Stan, is that you? . . . You don't know who I am?' She laughed softly. 'If you did, you'd be surprised to hear from me . . . Sure, I'll tell you who I am.' She paused, then slipped back into her normal speaking voice and all she said was: 'Surprised, Stan?'

Rollison heard the gasp at the other end of the line; and then the man hung up abruptly.

She said slowly: 'Now I believe he did it.'

Then she saw a different Rollison.

He jumped up, called: 'Jolly!' and, as Jolly came in, he motioned to the telephone and ordered: 'Call Grice. Ask him to find out who lives at the house with telephone number Chelsea 12431. Clarissa—' He bent over her, looking closely, imperiously, into her eyes. 'What's Waleski's address?'

She didn't hesitate to answer.

'18, Wilson Street.'

'Stay here until I come back, if you know what's good for you. Jolly—' Jolly was dialling. 'When you've finished, take a taxi and come to 18, Wilson Street.'

146

The last thing he saw in the room was Clarissa's startled eyes.

* * *

Wilson Street was between the King's Road and the Thames; short, wide, it had terraces of tall houses on either side. Half an hour after Clarissa had telephoned, Rollison turned the corner and saw a two-seater car, with the rear and sidelights on, a few houses along. As he drew near, the door of the house opened and two men hurried out, each carrying a suitcase. One was Waleski, the other was small and thin: Judith's assailant.

Rollison drove past and the others didn't look at him but hurried back for more cases. It was ten minutes or more before they moved off.

CHAPTER TWELVE

Night Ride

Rollison pulled out to round a huge double-decker bus which glowed red in the headlights of a car behind him and saw Waleski's two-seater, not far ahead.

They were approaching Fulham Palace Road; it was the first time he had seen the

147

other car since it had come out of Wilson Street and turned left into King's Road.

He slowed down.

When the two-seater passed beneath tall street-lamps he saw that Waleski was at the wheel. Waleski seemed intent on his driving and neither he nor his companion looked round. But that didn't mean that they had no idea that they were being followed.

Waleski turned left again, towards Putney.

Rollison looked at his petrol-gauge and silently blessed Jolly who must have had the tank filled during the day. He could drive through the night if necessary. He sat back, relaxed and comfortable, letting his mind dwell on Clarissa; and he smiled. Had he been told three hours ago that he would come to like her before the night was out, he would have laughed. Something in her manner when she had come round had touched a spark in him. He hoped he'd startled her by this swift move; and wondered whether she would stay at the hotel.

He doubted it.

Waleski drove straight up Putney Hill.

He knew the green Rolls-Bentley; he could hardly forget it after that morning. But it was difficult to judge colours by night and Rollison kept a hundred yards behind him. But he needed another car. He couldn't be sure of escaping notice while he remained in this one. There wasn't a chance of getting one but it was good to dream. Any old crock would do; the two-seater seemed to be going all out and didn't pass forty-five miles an hour. For Rollison it was snail's pace on an empty road.

They turned right at Putney Heath, towards Roehampton and the Kingston Bypass.

Woking—and Surrey—lay ahead.

If Waleski recognised the Bentley, he would probably go anywhere but to his real destination.

A taxi-horn honked behind him. There was nothing on the road except one of London's cabs, so antediluvian as to have an old-fashioned rubber and brass horn. Rollison pulled over and the taxi-driver honked again. He glanced round as it overtook him then saw a man in the back of the cab, pressing close to the window. There was a pale face and a pair of bright eyes and a waving hand.

Jolly!

Rollison exclaimed: 'Wonderful!'

There was open land on either side: Wimbledon Common lay under the stars. In the headlights of cars coming each way, couples showed up, arms linked; two couples sat on a seat near the road. Rollison pulled in just beyond them and the taxi stopped a few yards ahead. Rollison jumped out and Jolly came to meet him.

'Do you need me, sir? Or shall I take the car?'

'Go back to the flat in it,' said Rollison. 'And

149

make yourself a medal.'

'Very good, sir. The driver has been well paid and I think he will be satisfactory.'

Rollison was already climbing in.

'He'll do,' he said. 'Everything's wonderful and you're a gem. Off we go, George!'

The driver let in the clutch and jolted Rollison forward; and Rollison thought he grinned. The rear light of Waleski's car was nearly two hundred yards ahead now but the taxi had a fine burst of speed. Rollison leaned forward and opened the partition between him and the driver.

'All set for a night out?'

'Sure.'

'Petrol?'

'Plenty.'

'Have you seen the two-seater?'

'Yep.'

'You wouldn't like to trust me at the wheel, would you?'

'*I* wouldn't mind but it would be against the law, guv'nor.' The driver grinned again. 'You just give me your orders and behave like a real toff.'

Rollison laughed. 'You'll do. I don't want to get too close to the two-seater; I just want to know where it's going.'

'And the rest, guv'nor!' The taxi-driver took a hand off the wheel and raised it. 'I can use my mitts. Glad to, if there's any trouble. Life's pretty dull these days. Sure you wouldn't like

150

to pass 'em and force 'em into the side of the road?'

'You calm down and get ready to be disappointed in me.'

The driver chuckled.

They were speeding along the bypass and Rollison judged that they were travelling at fifty miles an hour. He smoked and watched. Now and again the two-seater was held up at traffic lights but the driver of the cab always slowed down in time to avoid getting too close. Sometimes three or four cars were between them and their quarry, sometimes none at all. They were too far away for Rollison to guess whether the men in the two-seater were paying them any attention.

At the end of the bypass they took the Guildford Road. By then Rollison was frowning, trying to guess where Waleski was going. Five miles farther along they turned off the main road along a narrower one. Rollison told his driver to switch off his lights; he no longer had to guess where they were going— he knew: Waleski was heading for Sir Frederick Arden's country home.

*   *   *

Arden Lodge stood on the brow of a hill, a large, gabled house, no more than a dark shape against the sky except where yellow lights shone at long, narrow windows. The cab, still without lights, passed the end of the drive and Rollison could see the two-seater, standing outside the front door.

The cabby slowed down.

'Going in, Guv'nor?'

'No, going home.'

'But, Guv'nor—'

'I told you to get ready to be disappointed,' Rollison said. 'I couldn't improve on this night's work but I could spoil it.'

'They might go on somewhere else,' said the cabby.

His sharp profile was turned towards Rollison; his expression looked almost pleading in the faint light. Heaven knew what Jolly had told him. If the man were Snub or Jolly, he'd have no doubt what to do but—this was a stranger with no reason to be more loyal to Rollison than to any stranger. And there was danger from Waleski.

'Have a go,' pleaded the cabby.

Rollison said: 'All right, I'll take a chance. Stay here, follow the two-seater if it leaves and let me know where it goes. If nothing's happened by one o'clock, give it up. Know where to find me?'

'If I don't I'll ask Bill Ebbutt.'

'Oh-ho,' said Rollison and doubts about the man dimmed. 'Be careful; they're armed.'

'Your man told me so,' said the cabby. 'You don't have to worry, Mr Rollison. I'm one of Bert's new drivers. Mr Jolly 'phoned Bert and asked him to be at the Oxford Palace.' Bert was a taxi and garage owner in the East End who often did work for Rollison. 'Bert's got 'flu, so he asked me to come along. You don't have to worry. I'll keep me lights off and follow them without them knowing I'm around. Done plenty of it in France but you don't want to hear the story of what I did in the war, do you? Trouble is, what are you going to do?'

'I'm going to take a walk,' said Rollison.

'Coming back?'

'No, you're in charge here.'

'Hope you get a lift okay,' said the cabby. 'I—Ta, Mr Rollison!' His hand closed round five one-pound notes. 'You didn't have to do that but thanks a lot. I won't let you down. Bert and Bill would tear a strip off me if I did.'

Rollison laughed softly and got out and walked towards the main road, a mile or so away.

*   *   *

He caught a bus after half an hour's walking, reached Guildford just after eleven o'clock, found an all-night garage, hired a car and was back at Gresham Terrace by midnight.

A light was on in the living-room and Jolly, who seemed to sense when he was coming in, opened the door.

'Made that medal?' asked Rollison.

153

'That is hardly deserved, sir, but—'

'Wrong. But you should have told me it was one of Bert's men.'

'I thought you would prefer to judge the man yourself as he was a stranger,' said Jolly . 'I instructed him not to advise you until—'

'He didn't. Well, it's been a good night. Waleski ended up—'

Jolly's right hand sped to his lips. Rollison broke off—and then looked into the living-room, the door of which was ajar, and saw Clarissa Arden.

*   *   *

'Well, well,' Rollison said, heavily. 'The lovely lady who couldn't take advice. How long has Miss Arden been here, Jolly?'

'For about an hour, sir.'

'Has she been difficult?'

'No, sir, quite placid.'

Rollison chuckled and Clarissa laughed.

Rollison went into the room, noticing that she had made up her face and most of the signs of her ordeal had disappeared. Her blouse was buttoned high at the neck, hiding the red marks and the weals. Her eyes were heavy as if with sleep but only a little bloodshot; there were no blotches on her skin. She was smoking and there was a drink beside her. She sat down as Rollison entered and for the third time looked at him through her lashes with her head held back.

'I'm beginning to think you're good,' said Rollison.

'Did you find out where Waleski went?'

'Yes.'

'Where?'

'You haven't found out yet,' said Rollison dryly.

'If we're going to work together, I think I ought to be in your confidence—don't you?'

A glass was warming by a tiny electric fire. Rollison picked it up and poured himself a little brandy, sniffed the bouquet, then whirled the golden liquid round and round in his glass, looking at her all the time.

'So from now on we're buddies?'

'I think we'll do better like that.'

'It's largely a question of whether I agree,' said Rollison. 'I might—when I know your story, Clarissa, and if you can convince me that all you say is true. That might be difficult.'

'I don't think it will,' she said. 'I've known for some time that someone is trying to murder my uncle. I've come to the conclusion that my cousin Geoffrey was murdered, that he didn't die by accident. I've been trying for weeks to find out why it's all been going on. That was why I spent so much time in Paris. I met Waleski in Paris. Would you like to hear about that, too?'

It was nearly two o'clock.

Rollison took Clarissa's key and opened the front door of 7, Pulham Gate. Then they stood close together on the porch and after a pause she said:

'Why don't you come in?'

'Fun later,' said Rollison.

'You don't trust me, do you?'

'No, not quite, yet.'

Her hand moved, sought his, held it; and pulled him closer. Her breath was warm on his cheek, her eyes glowed in the light of a street-lamp.

'I'm quite trustworthy now. I doubted you before. Waleski tried to kill me, as he is trying to kill my uncle and as he did kill Geoffrey. I don't know why; I don't know much about it; but I do know that I'm fighting for my life.'

'Very pretty,' murmured Rollison.

'So I've failed completely to convince you.'

'Oh, not completely. But there's more at stake than you, Clarissa. A nice girl named Judith and a lad by the name of Mellor, who—'

'Mellor!' She dropped his hand, and drew back. '*Mellor!* Do you know that brute?'

CHAPTER THIRTEEN

More About Mellor

She wasn't acting. One moment she had been pleading, using all her wiles and her beauty to break down Rollison's resistance; then, at the mention of Mellor, she had been shocked, filled with a repugnance which rang clearly in her voice. Into the word 'brute' she had put a world of loathing and contempt.

Rollison took her arm.

'I think I'll come in, after all,' he said and led her inside, closed the door and went to the drawing-room.

When he switched on the light, he saw that she was pale and shaken; the effect of Mellor's name was the same on her as it had been on Grice and Ebbutt. He mixed her a whisky-and-soda from a tray which had been left out.

She watched him intently without speaking.

'Here's early death to the villain! Sit down, Clarissa, and tell me all about the brutality and villainy of Jim Mellor.'

'He's—an unspeakable brute.'

'Who said so?'

'I say so. He—' She sipped her drink and sat down slowly; and Rollison was surprised that she flushed, as if at an embarrassing memory. 'I once knew him. My uncle had probably told

157

you about my hankering after the flesh-pots.'

'He called it excitement.'

'Anything for a new sensation,' said Clarissa, as if talking to herself. 'Yes, I suppose that's right. Life's unbearably dull—most good people are such fools, such bores. I suppose I was always restless and the war made it worse. I couldn't settle to anything afterwards. It might have been different if Michael—'

She caught her breath and jumped up.

'I'm getting maudlin!'

'You're becoming human,' Rollison murmured. 'I like it. You owe Waleski a lot, Clarissa. When he nearly choked the life out of you he scraped off that veneer of cynicism. Please don't put it back again; it only smears the lily. Who was Michael?'

Tears were close to her eyes.

It was late; she had been near death; she had been shocked and shaken; and so it might be said that she wasn't herself and had every excuse for breaking down. She didn't answer at first but closed her eyes. Suddenly she sat erect, raised her head and finished her drink quickly. Then she spoke in sharp, staccato sentences.

'We were engaged. He was a Pathfinder and didn't come back. You remind me of him. I couldn't think who it was when you came here this evening. But the way you behaved at the hotel—yes, you remind me of him. But he's dead, best forgotten. We were talking about my vices. Anything for a new sensation. That's really why I started to probe into my uncle's illness. I suspected that it was attempted murder. When my cousin died I think I was the only one who discovered that he'd spent a lot of time in the East End of London. I think he had your complex. He liked slumming—and new sensations. You do, too—don't you?'

'Yes,' said Rollison gently.

'So I went down to the East End. Oh, I didn't go as a ministering angel; it was a new kind of sight-seeing trip. I had an escort.'

'Who?'

'Does it matter?'

'Yes.'

'Billy Manson, the boxer,' said Clarissa and her lips twisted wryly. 'Another of my sensations. Ugly men fascinate me, so does brute strength, and Billy had them both. I told him I wanted to see how the poor lived. He was born in Limehouse and isn't ashamed of it, in spite of his fortune. He took me round. I was astonished at how many different people he knew. Criminals!' She laughed. 'I wonder if you can imagine the thrill I got when I first met a man who had committed murder and got away with it.'

Rollison said: 'I think so.'

'I almost believe you can. Billy did me proud but said there was one man in the East End I'd never be able to meet. Mellor. That was the first time I heard the name. It was impossible to meet him and of course I was determined to do the impossible. Billy was frantic, told me I was playing with fire—poor dear! He didn't realise that I like fire. It wasn't through Billy that I met Mellor, though; it was by accident. I went to a dance in Limehouse. It—it was dreadful! The crowd of sweating humanity—Oh, never mind. Mellor was there although I didn't know it until I had a note from him. A kind of royal command. Billy was to have taken me to the dance but he had a heavy cold and his manager wouldn't let him out, so I went with two friends of his. They shook at the knees when Mellor's message came and advised me to leave. Leave! I laughed at them and met Mellor.'

She fell silent again and Rollison gave her a cigarette and lit it for her. She hardly noticed what she was doing; she was re-living the meeting with Mellor in a scene which Rollison knew so well. A dance-hall, dusty, festooned with grimy coloured paper flags, crowded with Lascars, seamen, dockers, factory workers; beer flowing freely, rowdyism, wild dances— and one man who held a kind of court and whom everyone in the room feared. The only remarkable thing about it was the speed with which Mellor had won this position. Rollison had spent some time in the East End only six months ago and had not heard of Mellor then.

He asked: 'How long ago was this?'

'About six months. I met Mellor,' she repeated. 'I can't explain how I felt. It was as if I were meeting someone I'd known before and whom I knew to be corrupt. He was quite young. To make himself look older and more manly, he wore a beard. In anyone else it would have been laughable but in Mellor—I'd never met a man who frightened me before and I haven't met one since. It was in the way he spoke, the way he ordered others about, the way he attacked that girl.'

She clenched her hands in her lap.

'We danced, of course. He was one of the hold-you-tight type, sexy, domineering. A silly little tipsy girl was dancing with a glass of beer in her hand and she tripped up and spilt it over my dress. He seemed to go wild, snatched the glass out of her hand and smashed it in her face. I shall never forget that moment. He just smashed it *into* her face, cut her cheeks and mouth. It was a miracle she wasn't blinded. She screamed and tried to run away but he caught her hair and bashed her with his fist— and no one came to her aid. I tried to but they held me back. I *did* try.'

She sounded almost piteous.

'Yes, I'm sure you did.'

'She was unconscious when he flung her away. Her friends took her out. I was told afterwards that she was in hospital for a month. But—' Clarissa shuddered. 'It was

161

quite horrible. The first new sensation that revolted me. I walked out, of course. I haven't been back to the East End since that night and I don't want to go again. I stopped trying to find out why my cousin went there so often. I told myself it didn't matter and I suppose it didn't. I hardly knew my cousin. He was at school when I left England during the war and we didn't meet after that. I tried to forget the whole business but couldn't. It was so obvious that someone was trying to kill my uncle as well. So I worked on Waleski. I've told you about that.'

'Tell me again,' said Rollison.

She didn't object.

'I knew my uncle had business in Paris and he kept hearing from Waleski. I read one of Waleski's letters and saw the signature. It was an innocuous kind of letter, just saying that he was continuing the investigations and hoped to have some news later. I wondered what the investigations were, whether my uncle realised he was in line for murder. Waleski wrote from the *Hôtel de Paris* so I went and stayed there. He wasn't a difficult man to meet and—well, you've seen him. Ugliness still fascinates me. He wanted to get information out of me about my uncle; and he kept talking about a second son. I still don't know whether my uncle ever had another son but Waleski talked as if there were no doubt. Waleski'—she laughed, a curious, brittle laugh—'thought that I was interested because if a second son appeared I'd probably get little or nothing from my uncle's will. I didn't tell him that I couldn't care less. I pretended that it mattered. I was to go through the papers at Pulham Gate and the Guildford house, looking for evidence about this love-child and tell Waleski what I'd found. Then Waleski was called to London. I followed after a few days and he called me to-day and asked me to meet him at the Oxford Palace. He was disappointed that I hadn't discovered anything yet and I—oh, I suppose I lost my head.' She leaned back and looked at Rollison from beneath her lashes: the familiar trick; she was feeling much more herself now.

'I told him that he'd better be careful or the great Toff would discover his little game. He went mad. He was holding his cigarette-case in his hand, grabbed my hair and struck me with the case. That's all I remember, all I can tell you. Does it—' She smiled; yes, she was much more herself—'Does it tally with what I told you at the flat?'

'Near enough,' said Rollison.

'It's the truth. And I still want to work with you.'

'We'll talk about that in the morning,' Rollison promised.

'Don't leave it too late,' said Clarissa. She stood up and approached him, taking his hands. 'Have I bored you?'

'Terribly!'

'That's where you're like Michael: you won't be serious when I want to be.'

'If I were called on to advise, I'd say: think more about Michael instead of trying to forget him,' said Rollison gently. 'There's more than one man cast in the same mould but not a lot of women like you, Clarissa. I think we can work together. In fact, there's a job I want you to do in the morning. Go and get some sleep; you might be busy tomorrow.'

'Yes, papa.' She gripped his hands tightly. 'Why did you mention Mellor?'

'I think there are two Mellors. We don't mean the same one,' said Rollison. 'We'll see.'

'I think you're lying but I don't really mind,' said Clarissa. 'You've done me a world of good. Thank you, Richard.'

She kissed him, full on the lips—a lingering kiss with more than a hint of passion—and the soft warmth of her body was close against him.

'Why don't you stay?'

'I'd rather find you new sensations,' Rollison said dryly. 'Good night, Clarissa.'

She laughed and turned away—and the telephone bell rang, startling them both.

*   *   *

'It's Jolly,' said Clarissa.

Rollison took the telephone. Jolly would not have called here unless with tidings of trouble.

Judith?

'Yes, Jolly?'

'I've just had a message from Dr Willerby, sir,' said Jolly. 'Will you please go there at once?'

*   *   *

Earlier that night Snub drove a tradesman's van past the clinic, waved to Doc Willerby who was talking to a woman on the steps of his Nissen hut, and stopped at a garage not far away. He drove the van in, poked his head inside the back, rubbed his hands joyously and locked the door. It was dark; the gas street lamps gave only a dim glow. When he reached the clinic again, the woman had gone and the door was closed.

He did not go in at once.

He had no idea where Rollison was but wished vaguely that his own job was different. Being nursemaid to Mellor wasn't likely to offer much excitement. But Rollison's training and his own instinct made him careful. He made a complete circuit of the outside of the clinic but saw no lurking figures, nothing to suggest that anything was wrong.

He wished he had a gun; or any weapon.

A light glowed at one end of the Nissen hut.

He rang the bell and Mrs Willerby, a much younger woman than her husband, opened the door.

'Not another emergency, just an extra mouth to feed,' said Snub. 'Hope I'm not too late.'

'No, we seldom get to bed before midnight.' She stepped inside and the light from a room beyond fell on her fluffy hair and round, ruddy, friendly face. 'The doctor is expecting you.'

'And wishing he wasn't,' called Willerby from the lighted room.

But when Snub entered he put down a book and offered cigarettes. It was a small, comfortable, homely room and a radio stood in the corner, soft chamber music coming from it. Snub dropped into an easy-chair and clapped his hands boisterously.

'I've found just what the doctor ordered, Doc! A tradesman's van, nicely sprung, used for long distances and fragile merchandise, as they say. Borrowed a divan and fastened it inside the van. Mellor will hardly know he's on the road. How is he?'

'All right.'

'Did the Boss say why he wanted me to come along here?'

'No. He probably realises by now that Mellor isn't the most popular man in the East End. I've pushed the second bed in the ward near the window and there's a good lock on the door.'

'That sounds ominous.'

'I'm not exactly expecting trouble,' said the doctor, 'but I'll be glad when you've taken

166

Mellor away.'

'You were a fool to let him stay here,' said Mrs Willerby, coming in with a tray on which were three steaming cups of cocoa. 'Can you drink some of this, Mr Higginbottom?'

'My dream of a night-cap,' said Snub. 'Thanks, ma'am. Don't blame the Doc, blame the Toff—he's at the root of all the trouble.'

'Do you think I need telling that?' asked Mrs Willerby.

It was half-past twelve when Snub went into the ward. There was a tiny electric light on in one corner. Mellor was lying on his back and appeared to be in a natural sleep. The window was open at the top and Snub made a face.

'Must have fresh air,' whispered Willerby.

'Oh, yes. I'll rig up a booby trap and if anyone comes in they'll make a hell of a clatter.' Snub looked round the room, brought two chairs to the window and placed a glass tumbler on top of the erection he built up. No one reaching through the open window could fail to knock the glass off. 'All will be well if it doesn't fall of its own volition,' Snub said. ' 'Night-'night.'

He kicked off his shoes, took off his collar and tie and lay down; ten minutes later, he was asleep.

*　　　*　　　*

He didn't know what time it was when the

167

tumbler crashed to the floor but it woke him out of a deep sleep. He sprang up—and the glass of the window fell in. He saw the shadowy figures of two men outside.

CHAPTER FOURTEEN

Night Attack

Snub muttered: 'Here it comes!'

He was conscious of three things at the same time. Mellor had woken up at the crash and was leaning on his elbow, staring towards the window; a man, head protected by his arm, was climbing in; and the dim electric light was just good enough for Snub to see the second man, outside the window, threatening him with a gun.

Snub said: 'Good evening,' squirmed round and grabbed a pillow and flung it at the first man who fell back outside, arms waving; and who caught his wrist on a jagged piece of glass. Snub rolled off the bed and, as he touched the floor, heard a soft, coughing sound, as ominous as the report of a shot; it was either from an air-pistol which carried a lethal slug or a silenced automatic; and silencers weren't as good as all that.

He shouted: '*Doc!*'

For a moment he knelt behind the bed, safe

from a second shot—but he heard the 'cough' again, swung his head round and saw Mellor clutch his shoulder. Mellor's unshaven face and wild eyes were livid with fear. He was in line with the window, an easy target.

Snub yelled: *'Doc!'* again and sprang across the room, putting himself between Mellor and the assailant.

He felt a sharp pain at the top of his left arm but it didn't stop him. He grabbed the side of Mellor's bed and tipped it up. Mellor slid to the floor; blankets and sheets toppled on to him, the bedside table crashed.

A door banged.

Snub ducked; another slug went over his head. He made for the door at a crouching sprint, changed his mind and his direction and joined Mellor behind the bed. As he flung himself on the floor he saw the first man climbing in again; blood showed crimson on the man's wrist. Mrs Willerby called out: 'Be careful!' The door began to open.

'Careful, Doc!' called Snub. 'They're armed. Haven't got a shotgun handy, have you?'

Mellor was lying in a huddled heap, not moving but gasping for breath and the top of his head stuck out from the bedclothes. The wounded assailant was now in the room. He wasn't badly hurt for, in his injured hand, he held a knife as if he meant business.

The other man began to climb in.

The door opened wide, the doctor's arm

appeared as he tossed something into the room. It struck the first attacker on the chest and broke. Snub, peering above the upturned bed, saw a cloud of vapour billow up and heard the door slam. Next moment the first assailant began to splutter and cough, the second gave an explosive sneeze—and gas bit sharply at Snub's eyes and mouth, a gas with a powerful smell: ammonia.

Snub stood up, holding his breath. The two men were beating the air, the knife curving wild arcs through the vapour cloud.

Snub pulled the bed-clothes off Mellor, bent down and lifted him, grunting. His eyes began to water and he wanted to cough. Holding his breath, he staggered to the door as it opened wide. He didn't see Willerby but heard his calm voice.

'That's right—this way.'

He felt a steady hand on his shoulder, banged against the open door, then reached the passage. Glass crashed at the window: one of the men was climbing out. Snub wanted to get at them both but had to look after Mellor and his eyes were blinded with tears. He saw a pale shape—Mrs Willerby, in a filmy nightdress—and heard her call urgently:

'Darling, be careful!'

'He's–all–right,' gasped Snub. 'Where can—'

'This way.' Snub couldn't see the woman's expression but felt her clutch at his arm. He followed her blindly and knocked against

170

another door. 'Put him on the floor,' said Mrs Willerby and there was no hint of alarm in her voice now.

More glass smashed in the other room. There'd be no hope of catching the attackers.

Snub put Mellor down gently and reeled away.

'Just keep your eyes closed; you'll feel better in a minute,' said Mrs Willerby and hurried out.

*   *   *

Mellor, thanks to the muffling bedclothes, was hardly affected by the ammonia gas and a flesh wound in his shoulder was much less serious than the shock symptoms.

Snub telephoned the Gresham Terrace flat, bathed his sore eyes, then his own wound; it was no more than a scratch.

*   *   *

'I was afraid of it but didn't really expect it,' Rollison said. 'Sorry, Doc. And thanks. Did you recognise either of the beggars?'

Willerby said: 'No.'

'I think I'd know 'em if I saw them again,' said Snub. 'The lamp gave enough light for that.'

'It might help.' Rollison, looking as wide awake as if it were three o'clock in the afternoon and not the early hours of the morning, bent over Mellor. 'Has it set him back far?'

'He'll need careful nursing.'

'Dangerous to move him?'

'Not if he's warm and comfortable. You'll have to get him away from here, Rolly; I can't risk any further trouble. Either that or send for the police. Are you still sure that you're right?'

'Yes. Snub, go and get that van you've been boasting about and keep your eyes open. Our pals might have withdrawn to regroup their forces. Better have this.' He handed Snub an automatic. 'Carry one until this show's over or I'll be attending your last rites. Doc, I'm really sorry.'

'So you should be,' said Mrs Willerby. She was more jumpy now than she had been when the fight was going on. 'I always said that it's never safe to help Mr Rollison, Tim; you mustn't do it again. I can't stand any more of it. Especially for *Mellor*.' She looked angrily at the sleeping man—Willerby had given him a narcotic injection—and then at Rollison. 'We have enough to do without looking after swine.'

'That's enough, Peggy,' Willerby said gently.

Rollison smiled. 'I know, Mrs Willerby. I'll make amends and I'll have Mellor out of here in half an hour.'

'It's all very well to *talk*.' Mrs Willerby

172

clutched her dressing-gown tightly, glared at the bed again and gulped. 'But—but ought he to be moved, Tim?'

The doctor laughed . . .

Mrs Willerby had three rubber hot-water bottles ready by the time the van arrived. Snub backed it into the clinic grounds, then came hurrying in to say that no one was about. No alarm had been raised in a district where strange noises were often heard at night and the wise course was to pretend not to have heard them.

The doors of the van were open.

They carried Mellor in and put him on the divan bed where Mrs Willerby tucked him in with the hot-water bottles. There was something furtive about the operation, carried out in the darkness and in a hush which was somehow ominous. The purring of the engine seemed very loud; the roar as Snub revved it up was shattering.

Rollison sat in the back with the doors closed.

Through a circular hole at the back of the driver's cabin he could see the shape of Snub's head. Now that he was inside and they had started off, he wondered whether it would have been wiser to sit next to Snub. He would go there as soon as they were safely away from the clinic; but this was the danger area. There were no windows at the sides so he couldn't look out except through two small windows in the doors. He stood up, held on to the side of the van and watched the mean, dark streets and the gas-lamps disappearing, only to be replaced by others. Snub drove fast on the straight and slowed down carefully as he approached the corners.

Rollison thought: 'We should be all right now.'

He actually moved to speak to Snub when he saw a car swing out of a side turning and come in their wake. Brilliant headlights shone out, dazzling him. He backed quickly away and dropped his hand to his pocket—but he probably wouldn't need a gun; this was more likely a police car than one of Waleski's.

Snub called: 'What's up? Trailed?'

'Yes.'

'Is Mellor snug and tight?'

'Yes. I'll keep him steady; you shake 'em off if you can.'

'Right.'

Rollison knelt down by the side of the unconscious man, putting his arms across the divan to make sure that Mellor couldn't roll off. Snub swung round a corner and the divan shifted; another and it swayed the other way.

Mellor didn't stir beneath the bedclothes.

The bright light still shone into the back of the van. It disappeared as they swung round another corner then appeared again, casting grotesque shadows.

'They're clinging,' Snub said. 'Police?'

'Afraid so.'

'Have to see it through now. Hold tight.'

They swung right, then sharp left. The divan skidded and would have tilted badly had Rollison not been holding it. He wished he could stand up, to judge the distance between van and car. It wasn't easy to think and he'd never needed to think faster. If this were a police car, it was probably equipped with radio. Radio patrol cars throughout London and the Home Counties might soon be on the look-out for the van; the call had probably gone out. The chances of escaping were negligible, unless they went to earth somewhere near, stranded the van and hid Mellor.

With anyone else that would have been easy: Ebbutt's flat, the gymnasium, one of a dozen pubs or Bert's garage would all have offered sanctuary. But no one would willingly help Mellor against the police.

He heard a splintering sound and glanced round. The glass of the left side window crashed in.

Snub whistled. 'That's Waleski! Hold tight!'

A second shot struck the wing of the van as they turned another corner.

Rollison called: 'Get on to a straight road and keep there for a bit.'

'Aye, aye, cappen—we're on one now.'

'Go as fast as you like,' said Rollison.

He stood up and went to the smashed

window. The blinding glare of the following car's headlights made him narrow his eyes. All he could see was the sheet of light and the twin orbs of the lamps themselves; there was no dark shape behind. He stood to one side and poked his gun out of the window.

He fired, blind. Nothing happened. He raised the gun a shade and fired again. Still no result. The roar of the shot inside the van was deafening, high above the sound of the engine and the rattling of the chassis.

He fired a third time. One of the lights went out and the car swerved. He moved in front of the window and saw the dark outline of the car which was nearly broadside-on. He fired twice towards the driving-seat and heard the squeal of brakes as the report of the shots died down.

'Twist and turn about now,' he ordered.

'Nice work,' breathed Snub.

The van swung round another corner as Rollison bent over Mellor.

*   *   *

The car didn't appear again and they were soon out of London.

*   *   *

'Well!' gasped Mrs Begbie. 'Well, this *is* a surprise. And at this hour, too: I can't understand it. Who did you say you are? Mr Rollison? A friend of Sir Frederick's? Well!'

She blinked at the pale blue note-paper on which Arden had written to her and then blinked at Rollison who stood in the tiny parlour of the cottage. She wore a grey blanket dressing-gown, her thin grey hair was done up tightly in steel curlers, her eyes were bright. She was a small woman with sharp features and full lips—not a kindly soul, judging from appearances; probably an irascible old woman.

'Well! And *who* is the man you've brought? Sir Frederick doesn't say.'

'A young friend of his,' said Rollison.

'Young friend? Not a *woman*?' the old voice sharpened.

'No, a man.'

'Well! Well, I suppose I'd better see what I can do; but it's a long time since I looked after anyone who was sick—really sick. I'm not so young as I used to be, you know; my old bones don't like work. But, thanks to Sir Frederick, they don't have to do much. Bring him in, sir, bring him in. He'll have to have the box-room; but there's a window there. It's quite sweet and clean and my niece slept there only last Sunday, so it's properly aired. I can't do less than take him in, can I? But I'll have to think about it in the morning. I know what I shall do—I shall telephone Sir Frederick, that's what I shall do. I'll go and turn the bed down now. Mind the stairs, they're rather steep, and mind you don't bang his head, there's a nasty turn. And he'll have to sleep in the box-room—'

She went off muttering to herself.

Half an hour later Rollison drove away in the van. Snub was sitting in the parlour, drinking a cup of tea with Mrs Begbie and listening to what she was going to do.

Rollison pulled up half a mile from the cottage and watched the road leading to it. He saw no traffic, no one appeared to be approaching. He doubted whether Mellor would be traced there; if he were—well, Snub was armed now and had strict instructions to send for the police if there were another emergency. There were limits to what Rollison could do alone. He wondered whether he were justified in submitting the old woman to the risk of an attack from Waleski, whether the time had really come for handing Mellor over to the police.

Waleski meant to kill the youth who might be safer in custody.

But the murder of Galloway could still be 'proved' against him. Only desperate men would have made the attacks tonight; and if Waleski were desperate he would probably make a fatal mistake. Risk or no risk, he must try to lure the man to go far enough to hang himself.

178

Jolly, bleary-eyed but still dressed, struggled up from an easy-chair as Rollison came in.

'Sit back and relax,' said Rollison. 'You ought to have gone to bed.'

'I simply couldn't, sir. Is everything all right?'

'No one who matters is dead. The pace is hotting up and we may find it gets too hot. We really started something when we championed young Mellor. Any messages?'

'Only from the taxi-driver, sir!'

'Only!'

'He left Arden Lodge at two-fifteen, just after Waleski's car was put into the garage.'

'Hardly a trifle,' murmured Rollison and studied Jolly's lined face. His eyes were heavy with sleep but his shoulders were erect. 'Did you look at *The Times* yesterday?'

'Unfortunately I have done no more than glance at it,' said Jolly. 'Is there anything of interest?'

'Have a look at the *Situations Vacant* column,' said Rollison and Jolly turned to the desk to pick up the folded copy of *The Times*. He studied the advertising page carefully, suddenly started and lowered the paper.

'A first footman is required at Arden Lodge. Why, that is remarkable, sir. *I* could apply—'

'You can apply but it isn't remarkable and the job's yours. I fixed it with Sir Frederick

179

last week and arranged with *The Times* to get it inserted quickly. But that was before Waleski blew in. He's seen you—one of our mistakes, Jolly. If you go to the Lodge—'

'I don't think it can be assumed that Waleski is going to take up residence, sir.' Jolly showed surprising eagerness for a new post. 'It is true that we did meet but he is not likely to have described me in any detail to those persons— if in fact there are more than one—whom he knows at the Lodge. If it were possible for me to examine the situation there at first hand then we might well find that a logical explanation of Waleski's influence at the house will greatly assist in solving the major problem.'

'Ah,' said Rollison.

'Don't you agree, sir?'

'I think you might get your neck broken or a bullet where it will hurt.'

'One can hardly expect to achieve results without taking some risk,' said Jolly gravely, 'and, if I may say so, it is not your custom to think of the risks before the results. What did happen tonight, sir?'

'Risks came home to roost and I took others, not with myself.'

Rollison explained, briefly, receiving from Jolly an occasional pontifical nod. Then he paused, surveyed his man thoughtfully, touched *The Times* and said:

'All right. Take the job if necessary but don't

take chances.'

'In so far as the two are separable, sir, I will separate them. Is there anything I can get you before you retire?'

The clock struck six when Rollison got into bed.

*　　　*　　　*

He woke to a medley of sound and confusion of mind.

Bells were ringing, something clattered, Jolly uttered a word surprisingly like an oath, a cup or saucer dropped and broke, papers rustled —and the bells kept ringing: two different sounds, one low and persistent, the other higher-pitched and less regular. Then a door —his door—banged.

He sat up.

A tea-tray was on a chair by the door. A cup, in pieces, lay at the foot of the chair with several newspapers. One of the bells stopped. There were footsteps and then a door opened and Jolly exclaimed:

'Miss!'

He sounded both startled and alarmed.

Rollison sat up, rumpled his hair and yawned, eyed the tea longingly and wondered why he did not feel worried about that '*Miss*'. He pushed back the bedclothes and put one foot tentatively out of bed, glancing at the mantelpiece clock at the same time. It was five minutes past ten—not exactly a satisfying night's sleep. Craning his head to see the clock, he caught sight of his reflection in the mirror. It did not please him and he started to smooth his hair down as the door opened.

'Jolly—' he began.

But it was Clarissa.

She held the door open and stared at him— and then began to laugh. Rollison drew his leg back and pulled the clothes up. Clarissa went on laughing and all the time there was an undertone background of Jolly's voice. Jolly, of course, was answering the telephone.

Rollison resisted a temptation to smooth his hair a little more and ran his fingers over his dark but greying stubble. He recalled that unpleasing picture in the mirror and looked at Clarissa, who might have come straight from a Paris salon. She wore a neat suit of large black-and-white check which became her tall, slim figure; so did the white ruffles at her neck and wrists.

She stopped laughing, only to smile broadly.

'Why not be useful as well as decorative?' said Rollison. 'Get a cup from the kitchen and then bring me my tea.'

'Oh, it's wonderful!' She gurgled. 'K-k-kitchen—yes, darling, I will!' She turned.

'Bring two cups,' said Rollison.

'Yes, darling!' She gurgled again. 'Would you like a little poison?'

Rollison couldn't catch what Jolly was

182

saying; it was a long conversation and must be of some importance. Jolly was a past-master in the art of getting rid of importunate callers, either in person or by telephone, but he was having great difficulty now. *'Yes, sir; no, sir; I really can't, sir,'* came like punctuation marks in someone else's monologues. Yet he must be on pins to enter the bedroom before Clarissa could invade it again.

He failed, for Clarissa came back.

'No, sir,' said Jolly. *'Yes, sir; no, sir—'*

'Isn't he sweet?' Clarissa put the cups on the tray, picked up the newspapers and brought everything to the bed. She put it close to Rollison's right arm and sat at the foot of the bed, leaning forward to pour out. 'For the first time, I nearly believe in justice.'

'Justice?'

'Catching you like this, after last night. What could be fairer?'

'I knew there was venom in the woman,' growled Rollison. 'A little less milk and rather more hot water, please. I like my morning tea weak. I wish I hadn't advised you.'

'To do what?'

'Go to bed.'

She started to laugh again and tea spilled into the saucer of his cup.

'Sorry,' she said. 'Drink up; I'll be a good girl and sit quiet.'

She gave him a cup of tea and picked up the *Daily Cry*, a newspaper which thrived on

183

sensation. Although she pretended to glance at it, she was watching him out of the corner of her eye. Suddenly she opened her large black handbag and gave him a cigarette.

'Gasping for one, aren't you?' *

'No. Thanks. What's the matter?'

'I came to tell you that I meant all I said last night and now I take some of it back.' She gurgled; it was a delightful, husky sound, making her seem much younger. 'And this is a completely new sensation, darling. Yesterday you gave me an inferiority complex. Don't you feel well?'

'I'll feel better when I know who Jolly's arguing with.'

'My uncle, I expect.'

'Why?'

'He was in a foul mood when I left him half an hour ago and crying out for someone's blood. Probably yours. I don't know what it was about but he wasn't thinking kindly of the great Mr Rollison. I shouldn't worry about my uncle but—'

The second bell began to ring again.

'Is that the front door?'

'Yes. Jolly will see to it. You stay here.'

'I want to be so useful,' said Clarissa.

As she went out she gave him a merry look, showing a gaiety which astonished him. She was younger; or at least happier in her mind which made her seem younger. She had thrown off the effect of the attack with admirable ease and something had put her in high spirits. Was it because of what had happened between them last night? Or had the morning's events pleased her? Was she telling the truth about Arden, or—

Rollison stopped worrying about that for he heard a familiar voice, raised in some surprise after Clarissa said:

'Good morning.'

'Good morning. Is Mr Rollison in?'

'I'll see. Who are you?' Clarissa asked.

'Superintendent Grice of New Scotland Yard,' said the caller. 'Please tell him it's important.'

CHAPTER FIFTEEN

Shock For Clarissa

Jolly reached the bedroom before Clarissa or Grice. He closed the door firmly and turned the key in the lock. His hair was on end and he looked both ruffled and angry; there was even a flush on his dry cheeks and a sparkle in his doleful brown eyes.

'I am *extremely* sorry, sir.'

'Everything happens at once, doesn't it? Who were you doing battle with?'

'Sir Frederick, sir. He wanted to speak to you and I felt that as Miss Arden was here it

185

might be wise for me to say that you weren't available. He was persistent and somewhat irate. In fact, I felt that his temper explained his persistence. I did not get the impression that anything was amiss—or, at all events, not greatly amiss. Did you know that Mr Grice has called?'

'Yes. Let him come in and then pour me out another cup of tea, will you?'

'With your permission, sir, I will pour the tea first.' Jolly drew nearer the bed and put Rollison's cigarettes and lighter on the bedside table. 'Shall I—ah—shall I endeavour to keep Miss Arden out of the room when Mr Grice comes in?'

'Do you think you could without using force?'

'No, sir.'

'Then don't. What's the news this morning?'

'I am afraid there is a full but distorted account of your first interview with Waleski in the *Daily Record* and the *Echo*, sir. There is little other sensational news and both newspapers have connected the incident with the Mellor affair. In the *Stop Press* of the *Record* there is a report that a stranded car was found near the Mile End Road early this morning and that bullet-holes were found in the lamps and windscreen, together with traces of blood. There was some broken glass farther along the road, according to the brief statement.'

'Is the clinic mentioned?'

'No, sir.'

'Let us be thankful for some mercies.'

Rollison sipped his second cup of tea and motioned to the hall. Jolly spent two minutes tidying up Rollison's clothes and the dressing-table and then unlocked the door.

He disappeared and said stiffly: 'Mr Rollison will see you, Mr Grice.'

'He will see *us*,' said Clarissa.

'As you wish, Miss.'

Grice came in, smiling faintly; but there was an edge to his smile; he was in earnest, in no mood to be put off by airy explanations.

Clarissa looked fresh and fair and still highly amused.

'Do you two know each other?' asked Rollison.

'We're going to,' said Clarissa.

Grice said: 'You're in bed late, aren't you?'

'Is that an indictable offence?' inquired Rollison.

'Whatever kept you up might be,' said Grice. 'It probably is. Rolly, I've warned you that you're playing with fire. If you were responsible for that car smash in the Mile End Road last night, you're for it. I'm told that—'

'Oh, *no!*' cried Clarissa. Grice, who had appeared to welcome her, perhaps because he thought it would be easier to deal with Rollison while she was present, shot her a sour glance.

'Leave this to me, please.'

'I'm sorry, Superintendent,' Clarissa said, submissively.

'I'm told that you were seen in the East End at half-past two. Not long afterwards there was a car chase and some shooting. Where's your gun?'

'In my pocket.'

'I want to see it.'

'Help yourself,' said Rollison.

He pointed to his coat which was draped over the back of a chair but, in spite of his nonchalance, Grice worried him; as he had at Ebbutt's. Grice was deadly serious about this business. He would not let up; and if Rollison's half-made plans went awry, he would be merciless.

'*What* time was this shooting?' Clarissa asked humbly.

'Miss Arden, I asked you—'

Rollison looked at her with his head on one side and said: 'Grice was told that I was in the East End at half-past two last night.'

'But, darling, you *couldn't* have been.'

The 'darling' startled Grice, the rest of the sentence made Rollison sit up. Grice lifted the coat from the chair-back and felt the pockets and took out the gun.

'Why not?' he asked.

'Because he couldn't be in two places at once and he was with me long after half-past two.' Clarissa watched Grice sniff the gun. 'Mr

188

Grice, have you known Mr Rollison for long?'

'Too long. Rollison'—the familiar 'Rolly' was gone—'this gun has been fired recently.'

'Really.'

'Don't you think he's ageing rapidly?' asked Clarissa. 'He has such a reputation that I thought he could stand the pace but look at him and then look at me.'

In spite of himself, Grice had to repress a smile. 'Yes, he's getting past fast living! When did you use the gun, Rollison?'

'Last night. I drove out into the country and did silly things to rabbits. Clarissa, I dislike you intensely.'

'Never mind, darling,' said Clarissa. 'You'll feel better when you've had a bath and shave.'

'I'm going to take this gun with me,' Grice said, pocketing it. 'And if the bullets found on the Mile End Road were fired from it, you'll be in dock before the day's out. I've told you, I'm not fooling.'

'Oughtn't you to look for rabbits?' asked Clarissa, sweetly.

Grice said: 'And mind you don't get into trouble for conspiring to defeat the ends of justice.'

'Isn't that a marvellous phrase?' cooed Clarissa. 'Do you mean, am I lying? I wouldn't compromise myself for nothing, surely? I doubt if I'd have compromised myself at all if I'd seen Rolly looking like this.'

The gurgling laugh came again.

Grice looked at her darkly.

'Do you know where Mellor is, Miss Arden?'

Her high spirits faded as fast as the smile. Eyes which had been brimming over suddenly became hard, even frightened. She stood quite still and the change affected Grice quite as much as it did Rollison.

'No,' she said. 'I don't know and don't want to know.'

'Do you realise that Rollison is hiding him?'

She shot a swift glance at Rollison. 'Are you?'

'Grice thinks so.'

'If I thought you were helping that brute—'

'You'd tell me the truth. He is, so you'd better.' Grice drew nearer, holding the gun loosely in front of him, challenging her. It was perhaps the first time she realised he was really an adversary to be reckoned with and again the name of Mellor had shaken her badly. 'Were you with Rollison last night, after half-past two?'

'Until four o'clock or later,' she said slowly. 'But, Rolly, if Mellor—'

'Rollison is hiding one of the most vicious criminals in England. He is deliberately trying to prevent us from finding the man. He had some silly notion that Mellor is a victim of circumstances and not just a scoundrel. Get that into your head, Miss Arden. If you help Rollison, you'll help Mellor. If you want to be helpful to anyone, convince him that he's

190

making a fool of himself. He doesn't seem to believe me when I tell him that helping Mellor might land him in jail where his reputation won't cut any ice. This man is a killer and we're going to get him and anyone who helps him. Remember that, Rollison.'

Grice dropped the gun into his pocket and stalked out of the room. He closed the door with a snap and left Clarissa standing very still and looking down at Rollison, as if she were trying to read the truth from his expression. Rollison leaned back and opened his cigarette-case, put a cigarette slowly to his lips and fumbled for the lighter on the bedside table. Neither of them spoke.

The front door closed and Jolly's footsteps sounded outside.

Rollison called: 'Wait there, Jolly.'

'Very good, sir.'

It was astonishing that Clarissa's eyes should be so clear, her gaze so straight, her body so rigid. She *was* a lovely creature and could change her moods so suddenly. Was that natural? Or forced? The contrast between the gay, laughing woman of five minutes ago and this cold, purposeful woman now was unforgettable.

At last she said: 'Are you helping Mellor?'

'We shall have luncheon together and I'll tell you then. We've a job to do before that.'

'If you're helping Mellor, I'm against you,' said Clarissa. 'Don't make any mistake.'

191

Rollison shrugged himself into his coat, adjusted his tie and looked at himself in the mirror. The reflection was not displeasing; the shadowy image beside it—the memory of what he had seen an hour before—took the edge off any feeling of vanity. He was nearly forty; he had never realised before just how much that meant. It might be folly to allow Clarissa to make him feel old; it remained true that she had jolted him badly and he half-wished she hadn't come. Only half-wished.

Why *had* she come?

'Jolly!'

'Sir?' Jolly's voice came faintly from the kitchen.

'Get Sir Frederick Arden on the telephone for me.'

'Very good, sir.'

Rollison filled his cigarette-case, tapped the pockets of his perfectly-fitting coat and went into the hall. Clarissa was in the living-room, reading an illustrated weekly, and her head was outlined against the noose of the hangman's rope. She smiled up at him.

'Almost young again, Rolly!'

'I hope you fade fast before you're forty. How old are you?'

'How ungallant! Thirty-four.'

'If you can tell the truth about your age,

there's hope for you yet. Clarissa, be careful. I think you may be playing a very dangerous game. You heard what Grice had to say. He meant every word of it.'

'Wasn't he warning you?'

'Not only me. Grice is an able chap. Don't underestimate him and don't underestimate me. Even when I fail, Jolly always comes to the rescue! Why did you come here this morning?'

'I just wanted to see you. You did me good last night. I haven't felt so carefree for weeks. Must everything I do have a sinister significance?'

'No. My worry is that it might have. What was your uncle's bone of contention?'

'I don't know.'

Jolly said into the telephone: 'One moment, Sir Frederick, Mr Rollison is back now.'

Rollison took the telephone while Clarissa turned and studied the trophy wall; but he knew she was listening intently, that she hoped to gather the drift of what her uncle said.

'Rollison here,' Rollison said and pressed the receiver tightly to his ear, trying to make sure that nothing the old man said sounded in the room.

'Where the devil have you been, Rollison?'

'Out and about.'

'More likely slugging abed,' growled Arden. 'I want to see you.'

193

'Gladly. This afternoon—'

'This morning. *Now.*'

'Sorry, but it can't be done. I've an urgent job—'

'Confound you, Rollison; you're supposed to be helping me, aren't you?' Arden began to shout and in self-defence Rollison eased the receiver from his ear. 'And I want to know what you're doing, I want to know whether you're making an utter damned fool of yourself. I want to know—' He paused, then barked: 'Is my niece with you now?'

'*Clarissa?*' murmured Rollison.

Clarissa swung away from the trophy wall.

'You know who I mean—I haven't a dozen nieces,' rasped Sir Frederick. 'Is she there?'

Clarissa could surely hear him now.

'She called,' Rollison said.

'And you called here last night. Oh, I know what goes on in my own house. What the devil were you doing here at three o'clock in the morning, closeted with Clarissa? Haven't I warned you that she's a heartless baggage and that she can't be trusted? Are you going to ignore everything I tell you? My God, I didn't believe you could be such a fool! Keep away from the wench; she's dangerous.'

Throughout all this Rollison eyed Clarissa and beamed; and Clarissa, after the first shock, forced a smile but did not look gay.

'Do you hear me?' bellowed Arden.

'Yes, and I believe every word you say,' said

Rollison. 'I won't fall for the luscious Clarissa's wiles. Is that what you rang up about?'

'Isn't it enough?'

Rollison laughed. 'Yes, I suppose it's plenty. You sound in fine fettle this morning. Keep it up.'

'I'm coming to the conclusion that you're an insolent young pup,' growled Arden. 'Just a moment, Rollison.' His tone altered and was much quieter; Rollison could imagine how his expression had changed too. 'Is there any good news of the boy?'

'He'll be all right and I am sure we shall get him out of this fix.'

'I want to see that boy, Rollison.'

'You'll see him,' Rollison said gently. 'Good-bye.'

He put down the telephone and Clarissa said: 'Home truths,' and left it at that.

Jolly hovered about the door but Rollison motioned him away. Clarissa lit a cigarette and looked as if she wished she need not stay, that she didn't want to undergo the strain of the next few minutes, the inevitable questioning.

'Why does he feel that way about you, Clarissa?'

'We've never got on well,' she answered.

'This isn't just a question of dislike through getting on each other's nerves.'

She said: 'It's much more than that. He

doesn't approve of what he calls my carryings-on. He's a Puritan at heart and always will be. He worships money, I worship sensation and the two don't mix well.' She was earnest now and that was an unaccustomed rôle for her. 'It's deep-rooted animosity because I've never listened to his advice. That's a cardinal sin in my uncle's eyes. In fact, it's more. You don't know him really well—you only know a rather frightened old man who doesn't like confessing that he's frightened and knows that I know he is. He resents that. There's the man I know—the man who hates independence in anyone whom he thinks ought to depend on him. He tried to make a soft fool out of Geoffrey but Geoffrey resisted, and finally revolted, because he had something of the old man in him. That's why Geoffrey started this slumming; he couldn't think of anything that his father would hate more. It was the same with his wife, my uncle's wife. She was a pretty, vapid creature, fifteen years younger than he, lovely to look at but always needing a strong man to cling to. My uncle just can't stand independence in a woman, and—'

She broke off.

Rollison said slowly: 'At heart you hate him, don't you?'

'That isn't true. I dislike a lot of the things he does and I resent his contempt for me but he's not a man to hate, Rolly. I can imagine circumstances in which I'd be quite fond of him but that would mean being sorry for him and showing it—and he'd fight against it with all his strength. It's just a case of relatives of different generations who don't get on. He's even sore because I'm financially independent of him—he always thought that my father should have left my money in trust, with him a trustee, instead of leaving it to me without any strings.'

'How wealthy are you?'

'Even by your standards, wealthy,' she replied.

It was difficult not to believe everything she said.

*   *   *

Before they left, Snub telephoned; all was quiet at the cottage, and Mellor seemed to be on the mend.

*   *   *

It was a morning of sunshine and cool winds, when the countryside near London had a green loveliness and a peaceful beauty which made both Rollison and Clarissa quiet. The Rolls-Bentley purred along the broad highway, passing most of the traffic on the road, until they came to the by-road where Mrs Begbie's cottage stood. The road led uphill and the cottage was hidden for some distance by pine, fir and beech trees. The small leaves of the beech had a delicate translucence which contrasted sharply with the furry darkness of the firs and the shapely gloom of the pines.

The cottage stood close to the road, at the end of a small village. It was not a pretty place; box-like, with a grey slate roof and faded red brick walls, a garden that was tidy but where few flowers grew and those as if in defiance of the two small grass lawns. A rambler, covered with pink buds, softened the severe lines of the front door. A narrow gravel path, straight as a die, led from a wooden gate to the porch.

Rollison pulled up just beyond the gate.

'Ever been here before?' he asked.

'I've passed near, on the way to the Lodge. Why?'

'I wondered.'

He opened the door for her and handed her out. She looked at the cottage thoughtfully and shook her head.

'No, I don't recognise it. Why have you brought me here?'

'A little experiment,' said Rollison. 'It won't take long and it won't do you any harm, although you may get a shock.'

The front door opened and Snub appeared, waving cheerfully; even at that distance Rollison could see that Snub hadn't shaved.

'A friend of yours?' asked Clarissa.

'Yes, my amanuensis, doing a watchdog act. This has been a grim business, Clarissa.'

'Did you do that shooting last night?'

'I knew it was being done.'

'Won't Grice be able to prove your gun was used?'

Rollison chuckled. 'I've been mixed up in this kind of thing before, you know! Hallo, Snub, how are tricks?'

'Fine. The food's wonderful, the old dear can cook a treat.' Snub eyed Clarissa with unfeigned admiration; he was a most susceptible young man and had no hesitation in showing it. 'Visitors for the patient?'

'Miss Arden, Mr Higginbottom,' murmured Rollison.

'Not my fault,' pleaded Snub. 'It doesn't mean what it sounds as if it means, either. It means the bottom of a hill, or village, or something like that. How are you?'

Clarissa said: 'First Jolly and now Snub! I hope you know how lucky you are, Rolly.'

'Oh, he does.' Snub was earnest but his eyes were gleaming. 'I keep telling him and he's a good listener.'

'How's the patient?' asked Rollison.

'Sleeping again. The Doc said he would sleep a lot and we were not to try to rouse him. He had some bread-and-milk for breakfast, though. He'll do. Going to see him?'

'Yes. Where's Mrs B. ?'

199

'Shopping in the village—she really is a marvellous old dear. Still has all her faculties and she boasts that she's seventy-six. For some mysterious reason she's taken a liking to me and you made a hit last night. Shall I lead the way?'

'No, there won't be room for all three of us,' said Rollison. 'Just keep your eyes open, will you? I don't think we were followed but if the police were on the job they could do a lot by radio.'

He led Clarissa across the small, crowded room. In the sunlight he saw that it was spotless and freshly dusted. Clarissa didn't ask questions but followed him submissively up the narrow steep stairs which creaked at every tread.

'Mind your head,' said Rollison and she ducked where the wall jutted out.

They reached a tiny landing. There were three doors, each of them closed; the box-room was immediately opposite the stairs.

Clarissa lowered her voice, as if the hush in the cottage demanded whispering.

'What are you going to show me?'

Rollison gripped her arm.

'Mellor.'

He felt her muscles grow tense, although he gathered that she wasn't altogether surprised. The name had exactly the same effect on her now as it had before. She didn't speak as he opened the door. The bed was behind the door with the head against the wall; all they could see was the foot of the iron bedstead, a bow-shaped chest of drawers with a dressing-mirror in a rosewood frame on the top of it and a small window with gay chintz curtains.

Rollison drew Clarissa in.

He stood by the window and watched her intently as she stepped past the door and looked at the sleeping man.

She took one glance, no more, and swung round on him.

'This isn't Mellor! He's nothing like Mellor. What are you playing at, Rolly?'

CHAPTER SIXTEEN

Not Mellor?

Mellor stirred at the sound of her voice.

'Look again,' whispered Rollison.

'I don't need to.'

But she peered, much more intently, into Mellor's face. He looked tired; there was no hint of brightness or youth at his eyes and mouth, and his forehead was wrinkled in a frown, as if he could not throw off the weight of his fear, even in sleep. One arm lay over the bedspread, the fist clenched but not tightly.

'Of course it isn't Mellor,' Clarissa insisted.

'We'll go downstairs.'

Rollison waited for her to lead the way, and studied the homely face and the curly hair for a few seconds. Then he followed Clarissa, closing the door behind him softly. When they reached the parlour, she said:

'What on earth made you think it was Mellor?'

'It is.'

'Nonsense!'

'You didn't know Mellor well, did you?'

'I shall never forget what that man looked like.'

'A beard makes a lot of difference and this one isn't wearing a beard.'

'A beard doesn't make a sharp aquiline nose flat, like the man's upstairs. It doesn't make thin lips full and friendly. It doesn't make small, flat white ears stick out from the side of the head—I can't understand you. I thought you knew Mellor.'

'That's the man I know as Mellor—James Arden Mellor.' Rollison gave no emphasis to the Arden, just let the word come out casually, and watched her closely for her reaction. It didn't come immediately.

'He's not the Mellor I know. He—*what* did you say?'

'He is James Arden Mellor.'

She caught her breath. 'So that's it.' She glanced round, as if for a chair and instead sat heavily on a stool; but she didn't look away from Rollison. 'James Arden Mellor—my uncle's love-child. Am I right?'

'Yes.'

'And that's—that's what you've been doing for him? Finding his long-lost son?'

'Yes.'

'Didn't you know attempts were being made on his life?'

'Yes. That was incidental.'

'I don't know why it has shaken me so much,' said Clarissa. 'Since Waleski started questioning me, I've known there was a son. It amused me—call it malice, if you like. Uncle so strait-laced, so quick to criticise and condemn loose-living, with a bastard child running about somewhere. But after Geoffrey was killed I often wished he had another child. He's been so desperately lonely since then. After Waleski's taunts I found myself wondering whether uncle wished he could find the boy, whether he would like to acknowledge him. And I suppose he asked you to trace him?'

'Yes.'

'Are you sure it's the man upstairs?'

'He was taken in by some old servants of your uncle's who pretended he was their son, actually registered his birth. Then he was adopted by some people named Mellor, a childless couple of good middle-class standing. They were killed in the blitz when Mellor himself was in the Far East. The sticky part was tracing relatives of the Mellors who

203

knew the truth about the child—that they'd taken him from your uncle's old servants. They had few relatives and most thought he was a child of the marriage. But everything fell into place. There's no real doubt that this is the natural son of your uncle and the adopted son of the Mellors, the only one they adopted. Until I heard about the East End Mellor, I didn't think there was any possibility of casting doubt on my fancy. That's been done with a heavy hand but, although it makes complications, it doesn't affect Jim Mellor's identity.'

She said: 'Mellor is an unusual name but there must be hundreds of them.'

'There are but this isn't simply a case of a name. The East End Mellor probably killed the man Galloway. Yet my Mellor is wanted for Galloway's murder. See the cunning of it? The killer goes to earth, the police get hold of my Mellor's photograph, the other Mellor's gang convince the police it's the man they want and the police go after him. What's more scarifying, the Killer's gang goes all out to drive Jim Mellor to suicide, too. It's pretty obvious that Killer Mellor hopes my Mellor will be taken for him.'

Clarissa said slowly: 'It can't be just that, Rolly?'

'Why not?'

'You hardly need telling. If I could see at a glance that this isn't the same Mellor, others can.'

'You didn't spend enough enough time in the East End to learn their wiles,' said Rollison dryly. 'Except for a few close friends, no one ever knew Killer Mellor well. He was seen in public occasionally, as at that dance, but if anyone who saw him that night was questioned by the police, they'd swear they didn't remember what he looked like. Some would describe him as tall, lean, fair and clean-shaven, others as short, dark, bearded and stocky. The police wouldn't be able to make head or tail of it. He's never been through their hands, I doubt if they've fingerprints—in fact, I'm sure they haven't, or they'd have had him before this. The first time Mellor appeared to slip up was over the murder of Galloway. Then prints were found and there was other evidence to point to this Mellor. And the police naturally assume that it's the same one. They not only want their man for the murder of Galloway but for a lot of other crimes that will never be proved against him. They will be quite ruthless where Mellor is concerned and will take a lot of convincing that they've got the wrong man.'

Clarissa said: 'I'm sorry if I'm slow-witted. You mean, the police couldn't get anyone to identify the real Mellor but they've got this one's photograph and they'd be able to get him identified as the killer.'

'That's it.'

'I could swear that it wasn't the same man,' said Clarissa. 'I would swear it.'

Rollison said slowly: 'That's what makes you important. It probably explains why Waleski tried to kill you.'

'I wonder.' Clarissa wasn't convinced. 'Where does Waleski come into all this?'

'I don't know but I suspect he's a fence or a contact man. The Mellor gang gets a big haul and has to sell the stuff quickly. Jewels, paintings, *objets d'art*, costly furs—all worthless to crooks in themselves—and they can't be held for long. They're too hot. I'm told that none of the regular fences—'

'What exactly is a fence?'

'A receiver of stolen goods. None of the regulars, known to the police, will touch Mellor's stuff. They know that if the police caught them with it they'd be in a bad way. But Mellor had to sell. Waleski gets around a lot, travels to and from America and the Continent; I should say he's their contact man. Probably he's the brains of the gang after Mellor, or even including the Killer Mellor, who's a man of action rather than a planner. It was essential that a Mellor should die and the police should think the killer out of the way. My Mellor evaded the police for too long, so the others tried to force him to suicide, and sent a note to his girlfriend.'

'The Judith you mentioned?'

'Yes.' Rollison leaned back in his chair.

Talking was an aid to thinking. 'The note was sent as "evidence" that he'd killed himself, so that no one should be hunted for his murder. The overall object, I think, was to give evidence that the Mellor gang had been smashed. Thus the police would be lulled into a false sense of security. It hasn't quite worked out but everything will be all right provided the Mellor upstairs is caught, proved to be the gang-leader—and that can be done by false evidence—and hanged. That's all logical enough. But I don't know where your uncle comes in or what Waleski wants with him. He asked just for general information, you say?'

'Yes.'

'Nothing else?'

'I know you're not convinced but I have told you the truth,' Clarissa said.

'He didn't give you any clue about any particular piece of information that he wanted about your uncle? Apart from the lost son, I mean.'

'No, I think he was just stringing me along,' said Clarissa. 'And I told him about meeting my Mellor. He started to talk about the East End of London and the gangs, because there was an article in the *Continental Daily Mail* about them: I told him about the girl—all I told you last night. I laughed it off with him, but—'

'Waleski knows you can identify Killer Mellor, so wants you dead and that puts you on the spot.' Rollison was brusque. 'Better accept that and be very careful. Have you ever come across a man named Dimond?'

Clarissa hesitated.

Rollison said sharply: 'Have you?'

'Well—'

'This might be vital.'

'I have, yes,' said Clarissa slowly. 'It's a name you easily remember, isn't it? I met him for a few minutes at the *Hôtel de Paris*. Waleski had some business with him and said he was a diamond merchant. He made great play on the name—Dimond the diamond merchant.' She leaned forward, her voice pitched low, her expression eager. 'I remember him well, because he was so absurdly handsome in an unpleasant way. He spoke good English, but I thought he was probably part Oriental. Sleek black hair, rather sallow skin—handsome as some Arabs are handsome. Do you know the type I mean?'

'You're good at descriptions, Clarissa. And you've become a vital witness. You can identify Dimond, Waleski and the real Mellor, so we'll have to take great care of you.'

Clarissa said: 'Are you trying to frighten me?'

'No. To warn you. Waleski will almost certainly try again and next time might—'

'Succeed,' said a man at the window.

*   *   *

208

Rollison sprang up, turning towards the window. Clarissa exclaimed—and Waleski stood at the window covering them with a gun, grinning at them. A heavy footstep sounded in the passage; the door of the room opened and a small, wiry little man appeared, also carrying a revolver which looked too big and heavy for him.

'I'll succeed all right,' said Waleski. 'Watch 'em, Fryer.'

The little man's gun covered them as Waleski disappeared from the window.

*   *   *

He came into the room, still grinning, and the sun shone on his heavily-oiled hair and on the pale bald spot. His broad flat face had an evil look, his wide-spaced teeth showed. He walked with a swagger. His left hand was heavily bandaged and he held his arm up, close to his chest. He crossed to Clarissa's side and pushed the barrel of the gun against her nose with a jerk which hurt her.

'Not your lucky day, Clarry, is it?' Then he turned to Rollison. The grin disappeared, naked enmity replaced it. 'And it certainly isn't yours, Rollison. Won't your pal Grice be pleased when he finds the body?'

Rollison said: 'Yes, he loves chasing murderers.'

'Still clever, are you?' Waleski backed away, as if he were afraid that Rollison would push the gun aside; but that would have been of no use for Fryer was covering them both from the doorway of the little, crowded room. 'Grice won't have to look for a murderer, see? Mellor's upstairs. Mellor is going to kill the pair of you and then die of wounds. It's easy. We'll do the shooting, wrap your hand round one gun and his round another. The little guy outside will get his, too.'

'Ah,' murmured Rollison. 'Snub.'

'We got him with the air-gun,' Waleski boasted. 'And we'll finish him off with something more powerful. Where's the old woman?'

'Out shopping.'

'She knows a thing or two,' said Waleski and laughed. 'Feeling good, Rollison?'

'I've felt worse.'

'You'll change your mind. What a lot of time you've wasted, trying to do the impossible.'

'It's almost the only thing worth trying to do,' Rollison said easily. 'Sit down, Clarissa.'

'You stay where you are,' Waleski said, 'Dying will be another new sensation for you, Clarry. See where it leads you when you ignore an old man's advice! If you'd been a good girl, like your uncle told you, this wouldn't have happened.'

'You seem to know a lot,' said Rollison.

'It wouldn't be difficult to know more than

210

you do,' Waleski sneered. 'But maybe that's not fair.' He feigned remorse, shook his head, then grinned from sheer animal spirits. 'Better be fair, Rollison, hadn't I? I was listening in to your pretty piece just now and you've got it all right. But you didn't know I had a man watching the cottage, did you? I knew you had Mellor. I reckoned you'd tell the old man and take Mellor to the Lodge or here. I had a couple of other places watched, owned by friends of yours, where you might have gone. I knew Ebbutt and his mob wouldn't lift a hand to help Mellor, see. Got it all worked out, haven't I?'

'Not bad.'

'Not *bad*—it's hot, Rollison! One of the smartest jobs you've ever come across. And I'm good! I could have wiped Mellor and your snub-nosed pal out last night but I thought you'd be along soon. I didn't think you'd bring Clarry, though. Very obliging of you, Mister Rollison.'

Into a pause, Fryer said: 'We haven't got all day.'

'Why, so we haven't!' Waleski grinned again. 'Hear that, Rollison? We haven't got all day. It will take half an hour to get your prints on the guns and leave the evidence for old Grice, won't it?'

'S'right,' grunted Fryer.

'So we'd better get busy. Know where a bullet hurts most, Rollison?' Suddenly he raised his foot and kicked Rollison in the pit of the stomach; not hard, just enough to hurt. 'Right there,' he sneered. 'Then you can tell me if you've ever felt worse. Fryer—'

A sound outside made him break off: the click of a gate, closing.

Rollison glanced out of the window.

Fryer said: 'What's that?' and Waleski went quickly to the window and stared out.

It was Mrs Begbie with a shopping-basket over her arm. She made sure that the gate was secure, then turned and came slowly up the path, looking right and left, as if to admire the few bright flowers and the pleasant country scene.

CHAPTER SEVENTEEN

A Killing

Waleski kept close to the side of the window and hissed. 'Wait at the front door, Fryer. Let her come in, then bash her. Don't waste any time.'

He turned and covered Rollison and Clarissa. Fryer slipped out of the room without making a sound. Mrs Begbie, wearing a black straw hat, her old lined face lit up by the morning sun and her black cotton dress sprigged with little mauve flowers, paused again to look at the antirrhinums and pansies which grew in a small bed, half-way along the path. She bent down slowly to smell the scent.

Waleski said: 'If you open your mouth, I'll put a bullet inside it.'

Clarissa said: 'Rolly, you must—'

'Shut up!' Waleski growled.

'Rolly, it doesn't make any difference whether we're shot now or in five minutes.'

Waleski said thinly: 'If you open your trap again I'll put a bullet right into it. Remember.'

'It won't help to warn her,' Rollison said quietly. 'She couldn't run away, could she? Hold tight, Clarissa.'

She looked at him reproachfully, almost contemptuously, and then moved swiftly, grabbing a vase from the nearest table. Rollison snatched it away from her, tossed it into a chair and held her arms tightly. Her cheek was close to his and he whispered: 'We'll make it.'

Waleski said: 'You've got some sense, Rollison.'

Clarissa moved away from Rollison, disbelieving, her face drained of colour—and then she started. Rollison saw why, out of the corner of his eye. A hand appeared at the window and he knew that it was Snub's hand. He saw the top of Snub's head, knew that he was pulling himself up by the window-sill. Mrs Begbie, not looking towards the cottage, began to pick some flowers and place them carefully on top of her shopping-basket.

Snub's other hand appeared with a gun in it.

His face was grey, his eyes half-closed, he swayed on his feet; but he made no sound. Rollison held Clarissa's arm tightly. Waleski watched them narrowly, ears strained for the approach of the old woman's footsteps.

Then he glanced towards the window.

Rollison roared: 'Get him!'

The meaningless words were to startle Fryer. Rollison leapt forward. Waleski was caught on the turn—and Snub fired. A hole leapt into Waleski's forehead, over the right eye. He raised his arms and opened his mouth wide. As he fell, Rollison snatched his gun away. Fryer burst into the room and a bullet from Rollison sent the gun flying out of his hand. The roar of the shot made pictures and vases rattle and shake.

Snub swayed again and fell out of sight.

A single word sounded clearly from the garden path.

'Well!' exclaimed Mrs Begbie.

*   *   *

Rollison carried Snub into the room and put him in an easy-chair opposite Fryer, who was unconscious from a blow on the side of the head. Rollison glanced at the man, to make sure that he was still out, then gave his whole attention to Snub.

Snub's eyes were half-open and he was grinning.

'Where did they get you, Snub?'

Snub licked his lips and raised a hand to his chest. Rollison drew aside the coat. Blood was spreading slowly over Snub's shirt from a wound rather low down and on the right-hand side; not likely to be fatal. Snub raised his hand again and gritted his teeth; Rollison saw the ugly wound at the back of his head, not caused by a bullet but by some heavy weapon. Blood matted the curly hair.

'You'll be all right, old chap. Wonderful job.'

Snub grinned and closed his eyes.

Clarissa came in with Mrs Begbie close behind her, a flustered rather than frightened woman. She drew back when she saw two unconscious men. 'Well!'

Clarissa turned round sharply and said: 'Please hurry with the hot water.' She looked at Rollison as the old woman went out. 'How is Snub?'

'Not too good. Take the car and telephone the police, will you? Ask for an ambulance and a police surgeon and utter the magic words, "attempted murder".'

'The—police?'

'All safe now,' said Rollison. 'I'd have taken you straight to Scotland Yard, anyhow—the quicker your story is off your chest the better. Grice won't ask for more trouble; he'll believe the story of two Mellors now.'

215

'You ought to know,' she said. 'There'll be a telephone in the village. I won't be long.'

She hurried out, soon replaced by Mrs Begbie, carrying towels and a bowl of hot water. She put them down and went out, returning with a can of cold water and some cotton-wool. Rollison had opened Snub's shirt and blood trickled down the pale skin of his torso. He began to dab at it and Mrs Begbie snorted:

'Let me do that.'

'Better do his head first,' Rollison said.

'I haven't been a trained nurse all my life for nothing, young man. Get out of my way.'

Rollison said: 'Bless you!' and smiled at her—and saw Fryer's eyelids flutter. He moved across, gripped Fryer's coat-lapels, dragged him out of the chair and out of the room into the tiny kitchen. He dumped him down on an old Windsor chair, scooped a cupful of cold water out of a pail standing by the brick copper and tossed it into the man's face. Fryer gasped and straightened up, even tried to lift his injured right hand.

Rollison said: 'Now you're going to talk fast.'

Fryer gabbled: 'Sure, sure, I'll tell you all I know. Sure!'

*　　　*　　　*

Grice sat behind his large desk at New Scotland Yard, listening carefully and without

216

interruption. Clarissa, sitting on his right, saw the ugly red scar on his face which would have disfigured him altogether had it been on the cheek and nose; the wound which had left that scar must almost have blinded him. Rollison sat in an easy-chair, his legs stretched out, his voice quiet and casual. He told Grice what Clarissa had told him: all about the investigations and his suspicions; everything that he had guessed and that Waleski had confirmed in that careless moment when he had thought himself quite safe.

Snub was in Woking Hospital; Waleski in the mortuary attached to Cannon Row Police Station, just across the courtyard of Scotland Yard. Fryer was in a police cell, not far from the mortuary, and Mellor was still at the cottage with detectives guarding him and Mrs Begbie shrilly insistent that he should not be moved that day.

Rollison paused, to take a sip of water from a glass on the desk.

'Feeling happier, Bill?'

'I may be when I've heard it all.'

'There isn't a great deal more. Let's sum up as far as I've gone shall we? You'll agree there was justification for keeping Mellor away from you? I mean my Mellor, who was not the man you really wanted.'

Grice said: 'Legally, you'd get away with it. I think you were a damned fool not to tell me the whole story.'

'Wrong, Bill. Once you'd got Mellor, Waleski and his friends would have faded right out of the picture for a long time. While I had him they were on the go, sticking their necks right out.'

'You'd still say you were right if you could talk after death,' said Grice dryly.

'There had to be risks.'

Grice shrugged. 'I don't think anyone is going to prefer a charge, so forget it. You haven't told me what Fryer told you.'

'He fitted in some odds and ends,' Rollison said quietly. 'Mellor, the real murderer, is still in hiding. Fryer swears that he doesn't know where and thinks he's out of the country. Fryer's confirmed that Dimond was in the racket. Although Mellor killed his brother, Dimond stayed loyal. You can guess what he's like from that. He exported a lot of goods abroad and smuggled the proceeds of the Mellor robberies out with his goods. Waleski found the foreign markets. I told the Middlesex police about Dimond—I hope he's been picked up.'

'He's being brought in now,' Grice said. 'What else?'

'Fryer knows that Sir Frederick Arden is involved somewhere; just how, he swears he doesn't know. He thinks that one of the staff at Pulham Gate was fiddling with his medicine—giving him diluted doses, which would explain his worsening condition but wouldn't rouse much suspicion. Waleski was also working with a housekeeper at Arden Lodge; but what the housekeeper was doing for him he doesn't know. I told the Woking police—'

'The housekeeper skipped. There was a third man at the cottage who also slipped away after the shooting. He presumably telephoned the housekeeper and another servant in London—they've both gone. We'll pick 'em up soon.' Grice spoke with all the confidence of a man backed by the massive machinery of Scotland Yard. 'How much are you keeping back?'

'Nothing at all. You'll find that Fryer will talk as freely to you as he did to me. He's just longing to be asked to turn King's Evidence. Oh—he was the man who attacked Judith Lorne, of course, and who took part with Waleski in that shindy on the Mile End Road. Sorry about that.'

Grice said: 'So you ought to be. Miss Arden, whatever the temptation, lying to a police officer is not only illegal, it's foolish. I suppose you got rid of the gun you used and fired a few shots out of the one in your pocket, Rolly? The bullets we found didn't come from the gun I took from you.'

'Fancy that!' said Rollison.

'I told you to look for rabbits,' murmured Clarissa. 'I'm glad you still think there's something funny about this.' Grice glowered at her.

'Anyone who can be facetious after today's packet of trouble and after missing lunch ought to be mentioned in dispatches,' said Rollison. 'Bill, there are two urgent jobs. Find out why Sir Frederick Arden figures in this business; and find the real Mellor. Any ideas?'

'We'll learn all about them both before long,' Grice said slowly. 'I suppose you realise that things may not be as simple as you think, Rolly. Your Mellor may be quite innocent but may also be involved. How did he come to work for the Dimond gang? Does that tie up with the Arden connection?'

'It could.'

'So you're not going to talk?'

'I've nothing more to talk about,' Rollison said. Grice grunted. 'I hope I needn't give you any more warnings. You've gone about as far as I dare let you go—you'd probably be better under restraint. Miss Arden'—he turned to Clarissa abruptly—'are you prepared to make a statement as to what you know, sign it, and affirm it under oath?'

'Yes.'

'I'd like you to sign it before you leave. I shall want a statement from you, Rolly, too. You'd better dictate it.'

'After lunch,' pleaded Rollison.

'No. Now. Unless you care to come to the canteen—'

'Heaven forbid!' shuddered Rollison.

220

A detective-sergeant came in, was told to take Miss Arden to another room and write out her statement, and Clarissa was led off. Grice and Rollison sat looking at each other, Grice sceptical, Rollison mildly amused; and it was Grice who said abruptly:

'It's not over by a long way.'

'It won't be while Killer Mellor's still alive.'

'Do you think Sir Frederick Arden is criminally involved?'

'He could be.'

'Do you suspect anyone else?'

'Have a guess,' invited Rollison.

Grice stood up and went to the window, overlooking the Embankment and the sluggish Thames. Plane trees, growing from the pavement, spread their branches until some almost touched the window of the office. A constant rumble of traffic and clatter of trams came through the open window.

Grice said: 'Sometimes you're too deep, Rolly, sometimes nearly simple. You've a big weakness. Clarissa Arden is a beauty and she seems to have you under her thumb.'

'Ah,' said Rollison.

'You've told her practically everything you know—you had done so before she came here or I wouldn't have let her stay. Are you sure she can be trusted?'

'No,' said Rollison.

'Then why trust her?'

'The sweeter the bait, the bigger the bite.

221

Bill, I'd like you to set your financial wizards at work and find out how much she inherited, whether she's had any heavy losses on the Stock Exchange or anywhere, what people she mixes with apart from the Smart Set, how well she really knows Dimond and knew Waleski. Then, if you've really a kind heart, tell me what you find out. You might get to work on Sir Frederick Arden, too. I don't think the old boy has told me everything and he's very anxious I should suspect Clarissa of leading a murky life. Feel happier?'

'I wish I knew what you really think,' said Grice.

'I wish I knew myself.'

'Have you any reason to believe that anyone else, besides Arden, is in danger?'

'I don't know of any logical reason why they should be. But is Killer Mellor logical? Will he just accept his *congé* and retire gracefully or will he hit back? If he hits, who will he go for? Answer: Anyone who's responsible for his failure. How does that sound?'

Grice said grimly: 'Yes, you're on the spot.'

'And not only me. Clarissa, possibly; the real Mellor.'

'That brings a leading question,' Grice said. 'Are you quite sure that the man you found is the real Mellor? Could there be a mistake in the identity? Is the man we want really the missing son?'

'Doing well, aren't we?' asked Rollison. 'I

don't think there's been a mistake. I do think that the Arden establishment is much more deeply involved than we're supposed to know. Suspicion switches, as they say, from the old man to Clarissa. There's even a third possibility: another relative whom we haven't yet heard about.'

'What's your bet?' asked Grice. 'The unknown, the old man, or Clarissa?'

'I wouldn't risk my money,' Rollison said. 'But if I were you, I'd keep a watchful eye on my Mellor, his Judith, Clarissa and Sir Frederick. And I shouldn't lose any time.'

CHAPTER EIGHTEEN

Word From Ebbutt

'Now what are you going to do?' Rollison asked Clarissa a little later. 'Go home and make peace with your uncle or come for a drive with me?'

'Come for a drive with you.'

'I ought to break the news that we shan't be alone.'

'I was afraid of that,' said Clarissa. 'Grice and my uncle made you nervous. Who are you going to bring for a bodyguard?'

'You'll see.'

The Rolls-Bentley, green and shining in a

burst of bright sunshine, stood outside Botts, where Rollison had taken Clarissa for a meal half-way between luncheon and dinner. The chef, although officially off-duty, had fed them well. He had been delighted to see Rollison and as delighted to see Miss Arden.

Rollison drove to Knoll Road.

A plain-clothes detective walked slowly up and down the street, two men in overalls were working at a water hydrant and showing no great enthusiasm for hard labour. Rollison recognised one of Grice's men and knew that the warning about Judith had been taken seriously.

He pulled up outside Judith's house.

'I wonder why Grice let you get away with so much,' said Clarissa.

'So does he. The law is flexible when administered by men of common sense and understanding. One way and the other, Grice and I have worked together a great deal. The ice is often thin but Jolly's saved me from falling through with two red-letter exceptions. Yes, I've been jugged twice but they managed to keep me out of the dock.'

'Is it worth the risk?'

'Now you're becoming fatuous,' declared Rollison.

As they walked across to the house he saw another car turn into Knoll Road; and again he recognised a policeman at the wheel. So Grice was having him followed; perhaps because he thought there was serious danger for him, possibly because he was not yet convinced that Rollison had told him everything he knew.

'May I know who lives here?'

'Judith, the nice girl,' said Rollison.

Judith must have seen the car for she was half-way down the top flight of stairs. She was dressed in her green smock, her hair was untidy, her face bright; for Rollison had telephoned her to talk of good news without telling her exactly what it was. Rollison was leading the way and Judith did not see Clarissa at first.

'I've been longing for you to come! *Is* Jim going to be all right?'

'Yes, he's cleared,' Rollison said. 'Thanks to—'

He stood aside, for Clarissa to reveal herself. The two women eyed each other, tears rising to Judith's eyes, although she was smiling and happiness glowed in her face.

'Miss Arden,' Rollison finished dryly.

Judith sniffed. 'I—I can't thank—'

'Mr Rollison is revealing a new side of himself,' said Clarissa. 'This is false modesty; if there's anyone to thank, it's he.'

She took Judith's arm and they went upstairs to the big room. There dozens of black-and-white sketches littered the drawing-board and Rollison glanced at them and saw that they were drawn much more effectively than those he had seen when he had first come here.

'Genius popping out again?' he murmured.

'Oh, they're dreadful! When can I see Jim?'

'When would you like to?'

'Now!'

'It will take about an hour, if you're ready to leave in five minutes,' Rollison said and Judith ran across the room to the tiny recess, separated from the rest of the room by a heavy curtain, and disappeared.

Clarissa looked at Rollison with her head held back.

'You see,' murmured Rollison.

'Yes, it's worth the risk. She's sweet.'

'She's paid a visit to hell and that makes London seem like heaven,' Rollison said. 'There are all kinds of hell. Have you been thinking much about Michael?'

'Well—rather more.'

'Has it worked?'

'I can think about him without feeling bitter or desperate and wanting to rush off to find some way of drowning my sorrow. Rolly, you've already done me a power of good. I think you ought to marry me.'

Rollison raised his eyebrows slowly.

'Original thought. Most people would hate the idea.'

'Would you?'

He considered; and it seemed to him that she was in earnest although the words had doubtless sprung unguardedly from her lips.

She looked beautiful; she was beautiful. Vitality throbbed in her, made her eyes glow, made her lovely face radiant.

'I don't think I should hate it,' he pronounced. 'But Jolly will tell you that I am not the marrying kind.'

'I wonder why you aren't married.'

'Jolly's answer will do for that, too.'

'Proposal spurned?' she said lightly.

'No, deferred.'

'You don't really trust me, yet, do you?'

'No.'

Clarissa said: 'Michael didn't. Michael told me that he wouldn't marry me while he was still in the RAF because he would be afraid of what I would be up to while he was away. He could have trusted me, he need not have feared that. So can you.'

Her hand moved, to touch his.

Judith called: 'I'm ready!' and thrust the curtain aside. Clarissa tossed her head back and laughed.

*   *   *

Mellor's skin was clear, his eyes bright; he looked almost well. He sat up against his pillows in a small ward at the Woking Hospital. On a hard, uncomfortable chair in one corner sat a local detective—and at the window stood Clarissa, a little to the left, so that she could not easily be seen from inside.

Rollison tapped at the door and entered and Judith waited in the passage, her hands clenched. She would have rushed in but he had told her that he must break this news gently to Jim Mellor. Mellor said: 'Hal-*lo!*'

'Well, Jim. Feeling on top of the world?'

'I'm a thousand times better,' Mellor said and gave a rather excited laugh. 'You're Rollison, aren't you?'

'Yes. Who's been talking?'

'One of the nurses and the flatfoot over there,' said Mellor. The detective smiled affably. 'They have quite an opinion of you. I don't know how you managed it or even what you've been doing but if you yanked me out of that Asham Street room I'll never be able to thank you. It—it's damned hard, even now, to believe that I needn't have done it, that everything's worked out all right.'

Words spurted from him, as if he were making up for the last weeks during which he had said hardly a word to anyone.

Rollison said: 'You'll believe it, as it's true. Have you told the police everything you can?'

'Everything but I'm afraid it doesn't amount to much. I didn't really know Galloway, I'd just done some work for him—printing jobs—not a great deal. I went down to Limehouse on business one afternoon and—well, I must have been drugged. When I came round I was in the room with Galloway and there was blood all over the place. I must have been crazy to run away then but I was scared stiff. I felt pretty groggy, too, and there was a little chap who came in and offered to hide me. He said I'd had a brainstorm, and—no, it's no use,' Mellor said, and his voice was hoarse, his face strained. 'I suddenly found myself on the run—and then the newspapers came out with my photograph and I knew I was for it. I thought if I could keep out of the way long enough, the truth would come out. I know it was crazy, but—'

'Worry about it later,' Rollison said. 'Is there anyone you want to see?'

'Want to see? I'm longing to see Punch—Judith. My fiancée—that is, unless she's decided that I'm not worth seeing. She might—but I couldn't have written to her! It would have involved her in the mess, too. Wouldn't it? Have you met her? The police promised—'

He couldn't speak quickly enough.

'Yes, I've met her,' Rollison said. 'She's here.'

'*What*?'

Rollison turned his head. 'All right, Judith.'

The door swung open. Judith came slowly into the room, her eyes glistening, her arms outstretched, but there was a little hesitancy in her manner, as if this reunion were not quite real. The light in Mellor's eyes must have convinced her.

He said: 'Punch. Oh, Punch!'

229

Rollison went out and closed the door softly. Clarissa watched from the window for a moment.

*   *   *

'I'm glad I saw that,' said Clarissa. 'Thank you.'

'Life can be good.' Rollison went to the other side of the car which was parked within sight of the window of Mellor's room. 'She'll stay there for a few hours and the police will see her home.'

They got into the car.

'It's better without a bodyguard,' Clarissa said.

'Still thinking of wedded bliss?'

'Just seeing the glowing possibilities of it. Rolly, I think I shocked you.'

Rollison smiled as he switched on the engine.

'Do you? Jolly would find that hard to believe.'

'Confound Jolly!'

'That won't get us anywhere; he's become as important as my own right hand. Clarissa, there was one thing your uncle said which is completely true. That you would try to make me forget the job on hand, which would sink me. If you did that, it would. This job isn't finished yet. We've to find the real Mellor and find out why there were attempts made on

230

your uncle's life, why my Mellor was identified with the Killer, why so much has been woven around the Arden family, whether you're right in thinking Geoffrey was murdered. And we've also to decide how much of what my Mellor said just now is true.'

Clarissa said: 'Why, all of it, surely?'

'Possibly.'

'You don't mean you doubt him?'

'I doubt everyone, with the possible exception of Judith Lorne,' said Rollison, 'and I'm going to go on doubting until we know all the answers.'

'I give in,' Clarissa said, and leaned back with her eyes closed. 'What do you want me to do?'

'Help.'

'How?'

'By finding out who might want to see your uncle dead. And who will benefit, enough to make murder worth while. Do for me pretty well what you were doing for Waleski but don't concentrate on the long-lost son any longer. And if you doubt whether I'm justified in keeping my eye on the ball, think over this one. If there is any other beneficiary under the will likely to have benefited from Geoffrey Arden's death, and who would also want the real Mellor dead, then Jim's still in danger. Pry and probe, as deeply as you can. Remember there could even be a second love-child.'

'Oh, no!'

'I said, could be.'

'I'll see what I can find out,' Clarissa promised slowly. 'Rolly, if I succeed—' she paused.

'Yes.'

'It doesn't matter.'

They did not talk again until they reached Gresham Terrace. The police car followed them all the way.

*   *   *

As Rollison turned the corner into the Terrace he saw an antiquated Ford drawn up outside Number 22g. The old Ford seldom penetrated the West End of London and when it did it was because Bill Ebbutt had urgent business with the Toff. In that car most of Bill's young hopefuls travelled to their early bouts—until such time as they could afford to run their own cars and pay their own managers, when most of them forgot Bill. Billy Manson had been one of those—and Rollison thought of the heavyweight champion, glanced at Clarissa, who smiled and said:

'What have I done wrong now?'

'You're all right. Did Billy ever talk to you about one William Ebbutt?'

'No.'

'You'd better come and meet him,' Rollison said; 'it will be another new sensation.'

232

He glanced at her face and wished he hadn't said that; for her smile disappeared and a bleak look replaced it. There seemed to be a barrier between them as they went up to the top floor. She was aloof, distant and withdrawn—much more like the woman he had met at Pulham Gate.

For once Jolly did not open the door.

Rollison let himself in and ushered Clarissa into the hall and Ebbutt's unlovely voice immediately made itself heard.

'That's wot I would'a done to 'im, Mr Jolly. Cut 'is 'eart aht. To talk abaht one o' my boys that way. Won on a foul, did 'e? Not in all yer nacheral!'

'Indeed,' murmured Jolly.

'You see what I mean,' said Rollison.

Clarissa forced a smile. 'Yes, I see. Rolly, I think I will go and have a talk with my uncle. I'll let you know if I find out anything that might help. I'm still glad I saw Judith and Jim.'

'Now, Clarissa—'

She smiled again and, although there was beauty, there was no life with it. She turned and hurried out of the flat and down the stairs, her movements smooth and graceful, her head held high. Rollison stood with a hand on the door, watching her, but she didn't look round.

Ebbutt was still talking, Jolly murmuring occasional platitudes.

The downstairs door closed.

Rollison turned and went into the living-room.

Ebbutt was sitting in an armchair, his back to the trophy wall, while Jolly stood with a duster in his hand, occasionally moving a paper off the desk and dusting beneath it. Ebbutt overflowed in the big chair, a dazzling sight. He wore a check suit in a larger, louder check than Clarissa's, a yellow bow tie and a pair of brightly shining brown boots of a yellowish-brown colour. His thin hair, quite grey, was plastered over his cranium and there was a beautiful quiff at the front; and by his side was a tankard of beer.

'Hallo, Bill,' said Rollison.

'Why, Mr Ar!' Ebbutt placed his hands on the arms of the chair and started to get up.

'Stay where you are, Bill. Beer, Jolly.'

'Yes, sir.'

Bill sank back with an audible sigh but did not speak again immediately. He licked his lips, took another swig of his beer and looked as shamefaced as he was ever likely to look. Jolly came in with another tankard of foaming beer, while Ebbutt ran his hand over his mouth, as if that would help to clear his mind, and muttered:

'All I can say is, I'm sorry, Mr Ar—I reely am sorry. I wouldn't 'ave 'ad it 'appen for a fortune. I 'opes yer believe that, Mr Ar. You ought to 'ave 'eard my Lil. Give me a proper

234

basinful, she did, said I oughta've known better than fink you would get up to any funny business like 'elping the Killer. I'm sorry, Mr Ar, that's it and all abaht it.'

'Don't be an ass. You did what you thought you ought to do. What's the news, Bill?'

'Why, 'aven't you 'eard?'

'I don't think so. What is it?'

'Why, *Mellor's* arahnd. I got the tickle on the grapevine, s'mornin'. 'E's arahnd, an' there ain't any fink the matter wiv' 'im, so the man you 'ad couldn't 've bin 'im, could 'e? I just want ter say, Mr Ar, if there's anyfink I can do to 'elp, it's as good as done. I'll stop 'im gettin' you if it's the last fing I do.'

Rollison said mildly: 'So he's after me, is he?'

'S'right,' said Ebbutt, nodding ponderously. 'Says 'e's gonna kill you, Mr Ar. 'E spread the word arahnd; that's why I came—to give yer the tip. Don't forget, that man's a killer.'

CHAPTER NINETEEN

Challenge

Rollison drank some beer, Ebbutt banged his empty tankard down on the desk and Jolly looked at Rollison as if asking permission to speak. Rollison went to the trophy wall and let the noose of the hempen rope slide through his fingers.

'Yes, Jolly?'

'The man Mellor telephoned, sir, just before Mr Ebbutt arrived.'

Ebbutt cried: 'Wot?'

'And what did the man Mellor have to say?' asked Rollison.

'He intimated what Mr Ebbutt has already mentioned. He requested me to tell you that if it is the last thing he does, he will get—ah—even with you about this. He seemed sober, sir.'

'Sober!' choked Ebbutt.

'What was his voice like?'

'I was rather surprised, I must confess. He spoke like an educated man. He did not rant, as might have been expected.' Jolly contrived to bring chillness into the atmosphere of the living-room—the stillness that was Mellor. 'He did not threaten wildly or go into any detail. I found the message disturbing and I do hope you will be extremely careful.'

'You gotta be,' Ebbutt said earnestly. 'You just gotta be.'

'An educated man,' murmured Rollison. 'Yes, that fits in.'

'Fits in wiv wot?' asked Ebbutt.

'A stray notion that's been running through my mind,' Rollison said. 'Bill, there's a job you can do for me right away—get it started as soon as you reach home and finish before the night's out.'

'Just say the word, Mr Ar; just say the word!'

'That's what I want you to do. Use the grapevine and tell Mellor that I'd like to meet him. He can name the place and the time and he'll probably want to make conditions. If you get a message from him, let me have it quickly.'

Ebbutt sat there with his mouth agape.

'Are you sure that is wise, sir?' Jolly was edgy and anxious.

'If you arst me, it's crazy,' said Ebbutt emphatically. 'Mr Ar, why don't you berlieve me when I say that Mellor's bad? Bad as they come! If you want to meet 'im at any place 'e'd do yer in and larf like 'ell while 'e was doin' it. Don't you go seein' the Killer.'

'Try it out, Bill, will you?'

'Well—'

'The last time I wanted you to do something for—'

'Nar, don't bring that up, Mr Ar. I shan't forget it in a n'urry. I've warned yer, that man's poison. But if you hinsist, I'll spread the word arahnd. There's one thing.' Ebbutt sniffed and seemed relieved. 'I don't suppose 'e'll send any reply. 'E'll fink it's a trap. If 'e does, don't take no chances, Mr Ar. Anyfink else?'

'Not now, Bill; but there will be if we get an answer. Have one for the road?'

'No, I don't think I will. I don't like drinkin'

237

much before drivin', not even that watery stuff. Where'd yer get the beer from, Mr Jolly? When you run that barrel dry, let me know and I'll fix some real stuff. You'll know you are drinking beer then.' He heaved himself out of his chair. 'Lil said I was to say 'allo, Mr Ar.'

'Give her my love,' said Rollison.

Ebbutt chuckled. 'That'll please 'er, that will. Tickle 'er to deaf. She'll tell all the Harmy abaht it, Mr Ar; they'll be praying for you before you know where you are. But Lil's orl right when she's aht've that Salvation Harmy uniform. Not that I'm *agenst* the Harmy. Cheerioh, you two!'

Jolly let him out.

Rollison handled the hangman's rope again and was holding it lightly when Jolly returned. Jolly's movements were slow and precise—a sure sign that a matter lay heavily upon his mind and he was not quite sure how to get it off.

'I'll buy it,' Rollison encouraged.

'Thank you, sir. How badly hurt is Mr Higginbottom?'

'He'll pull through.'

'And so will Mellor, I understand,' said Jolly. 'Mr Rollison, I beg you to take this suggestion seriously. You may not have solved the whole problem but you have found Mellor and carried out your obligation to Sir Frederick. The police are now aware that attempts have been—or may have been—made on his life and they both can and should protect him. We have escaped lightly, in view of the nature of the opposition. Haven't we done enough?'

'No,' said Rollison.

'Forgive my insistence, sir, but why not? I beg you not to assume a moral obligation which isn't yours. There is no need to carry on this feud with Mellor. His threats have to be treated with respect but with ordinary caution no harm will befall you. On the other hand, if you were to meet him or if you continue with the case, then it is very likely that you will get hurt. I don't think the circumstances justify that.'

'You're probably right.'

'Then why fly in the face of Providence, sir?'

Rollison smiled faintly.

'I want to know whether Miss Arden is as bad as Mellor, Jolly. I don't know any other way of finding out. It has become a personal issue.'

'In that case, sir,' said Jolly slowly, 'there is no more to be said about the matter. Have you yet informed Sir Frederick of the success of your mission?'

'I'm going to see him now,' said Rollison.

*   *   *

Was he going to see Arden? Or Clarissa? He would have made the journey whether

239

Clarissa were at Pulham Gate or not, whether he had met her or not, but that was begging the question. Did he want to see Clarissa or Arden? As Rollison threaded his way through the West End traffic he tried to answer it; and he wanted to see Clarissa. He wanted to find out what had passed through her mind when she had left him; why the light-hearted thrust about another new sensation had affected her so deeply.

Which was the real Clarissa? The first woman he had met? The new woman who had been born after Waleski's attack on her? Or some unknown creature—someone he didn't know and only vaguely suspected to exist?

Had she fooled him completely by her lightness and her gaiety, her surprising lapses into sentiment?

He turned into Pulham Gate. Two or three cars were pulled up near Number 7 but not Clarissa's. A policeman strolled along and reminded him of the attempt to kidnap him. Mellor had wanted to see him then, doubtless wanted to see him again, or he would not have made that call or spread his threats of vengeance through the grapevine—that tenuous telepathic communication system which ranged all over the East End. By it, a thing which happened in one locality was known in all within half an hour—except to the police.

A footman, William, opened the door.

240

'Good evening, sir.'

'Good evening,' said Rollison. 'Is Sir Frederick up?'

'I'm afraid—I'm afraid he's had a serious relapse, sir. The doctor is with him now. I believe that he has asked for you: the butler telephoned your flat a few minutes ago. Will you come straight up, please?'

*   *   *

Rollison passed him and hurried up the stairs. All the doors of Arden's suite were closed. He went into the study. The door leading to the bedroom was open. He stepped through. He could see the foot of Arden's big double bed and the doctor bending over it. Rollison waited until the doctor straightened up and caught sight of him.

They had met before and recognition was mutual.

'Come in, will you?' The doctor was elderly, tall, ruddy-faced—and grave.

Arden lay on his back, his lips nose and ears blue, his breathing stertorous. On the bedside table was a hypodermic syringe, on the foot of the bed the doctor's case, open, showing its chromium contents. No one else was in the room.

Rollison whispered: 'What happened?'

'I'm told there was a quarrel.'

'Who with?'

'His niece.'

'Can you pull him round?'

'I can't. He might do it himself. He ought to have been dead months ago by most standards. There's no telling with the heart, though, and this man wants to live desperately.' The doctor smoothed his thinning hair. 'He was asking for you all the time. You can probably help him more than I.'

'Is Miss Arden still here, do you know?'

'She drove off as I arrived.'

Throughout all this the old man's eyes remained closed, his blue-veined hands lay motionless on the bedclothes. The doctor moved away from the bed and washed the hypodermic syringe at the hand-basin.

'Have you any good news for him? He thinks you may have.'

'Yes.'

'I should let him know as soon as he comes round,' said the doctor. 'Oh, yes, he'll come round, if only for a little while. This is his third serious attack and they don't usually get through more than two.' He smiled faintly. 'I like a fighter!'

'Yes.'

Rollison sat on the side of the bed and looked into the thin face, the prominent, bony nose, the slack, bluish lips. He thought that the blue tinge was less evident than it had been when he had come in; certainly the breathing seemed a little easier.

242

'How long will it be before he comes round?'

'Five minutes—or five hours. There's nothing more I can do. Are you free to stay here?'

'Yes.'

'I'll tell the butler and send a nurse,' said the doctor. 'And I'll be back in about an hour and a half. You can give him a spot of brandy. There's some on the table.'

Rollison, left alone with Arden, stood up and went to the study. The drawers of the desk were open—that was unusual. Some papers, seared with age, were spread about the desk; one was on the floor. He picked it up. It was a marriage certificate. Among the papers were birth certificates, including one of the dead Geoffrey.

Had Arden made a rapid search for some paper? Or had someone else been here? Clarissa—doing what Arden had asked of her? He picked up a sheet of pale blue note-paper. That, and the fact that she had listened at the door and knew Waleski, were the reasons for suspecting that she had not yet told all the truth. His feelings were unimportant. The truth must come first, everything else later—if he lived to discover it. How had Waleski got that paper? Why had she really waited at the door? What relationship had there been between her and Waleski?

He peeped into the bedroom. Arden hadn't

moved but the blue tinge was much less marked.

Rollison closed the door and took the telephone off its cradle, dialled Whitehall 1212 and asked for Grice. He had to hold on for several minutes. He looked at the photographs of Arden's wife and Geoffrey—who had been burned to death, leaving only a few shreds of clothes on the flesh, a ring and a watch to show who he had been.

Someone passed along the passage and the bedroom door opened. It would happen just then. A door closed softly, then the passage door opened and the butler appeared.

'Have you everything you want, sir?'

'Yes, thanks . . . Oh, Grice.' Rollison paused, as Grice spoke and the butler went out. He lowered his voice: the man might be listening. 'Grice, have you found out anything about Clarissa Arden's affairs?'

'Yes,' said Grice. 'She's no motive for wanting Arden dead—no money motive, anyhow.'

'So she's really wealthy?'

'She's worth a cool half-million.'

'Thanks. What about Arden?'

'He's in a very sound position; there's never been a whisper against his good faith. Where are you?'

'At his home. He's had another attack, quite a natural one, I'm told.' He didn't want Grice here yet; no purpose would be served by making him suspicious. 'I'll let you know what happens. Anything else?'

'A nark tells us that the other Mellor is gunning for you. Be careful.'

'Thanks. I'll be seeing you,' Rollison said.

He went back to the bedroom. Arden's right hand had moved a few inches and his left hand was twitching. Rollison was longing to smoke. He went into the study and lit a cigarette but drew only half a dozen times before he put it out and returned to the bedroom.

Arden's eyes were opening and he muttered something unintelligible. Rollison sat on the bed, and spoke quietly.

'Rollison's here.'

The old eyes opened again, closed, opened in a fixed stare; he looked as if he had difficulty in focusing and his right hand fluttered towards the bedside table. His glasses were there. Rollison picked them up, unfolded them and put them on. Arden muttered a word that might have been 'Thanks'. Rollison gave him a teaspoonful of brandy and he gulped it down weakly and licked his lips as if that needed all his strength.

Then Arden said in a clear voice; 'I want to see that boy.'

Rollison spoke clearly.

'You will. He's quite safe. Quite free. He'll come and see you soon.'

A claw-like hand shot out and gripped

Rollison's arm with surprising strength. Behind the thick lenses of the glasses, Arden's eyes were very direct and bright.

'Is that—the *truth*?'

'Yes. I've seen him and seen the police. He isn't the man they want. It was a case of mistaken identity. You needn't worry about Jim any more.'

Arden said: 'Thank God!'

He closed his eyes again but didn't move and didn't take his hand away from Rollison's arm. Rollison eased his position a little. Arden's hand was very cold; his breathing was still heavy but there was a great change in him. A smile played about the corners of his lips, the strain at his eyes was gone, his forehead was less wrinkled.

'Look after him, Rollison.'

'You'll be able to do that yourself.'

'Nonsense!' There was more strength in the frail voice. 'Nonsense. Haven't much longer. I—Rollison. *Rollison!*' He sat up, alarm sprang into his voice, all ease had gone. 'My study—what did she take? *What did she take?*'

'What did who take?' Rollison asked heavily.

'Clarissa. Clarissa, the besom! I caught her going through my desk. She thought I was asleep. *What did she take?*'

'What could she have taken that matters?'

'Those lying letters.'

'What letters?'

'They were full of lies, full of lies. I was a

fool to pay anything, to—Rollison, go into the study! The top drawer of the desk. Open it. Pull it right out. There is a false back, worked by a spring. You know the kind. There are some letters there. Lying letters. Blackmail letters. See if—see if she took them.'

Rollison said: 'Why worry about it now?'

'*Go and see!*' cried Arden. 'I caught her at the desk. I struck her. I told her what she was—a loose woman, a Jezebel, a Delilah. I hate her, Rollison, and she hates me. I'm sure she hates me. Go and look in that desk!'

Rollison said: 'All right.'

He wished the doctor were here or the nurse would come; he didn't know what would happen to Arden if the letters were missing; and a fourth attack might be fatal. Less than half an hour had passed since the doctor had left; he wasn't likely to be back yet. Where was that nurse? Was there any way of making sure that the old man didn't suffer another shock?

'Hurry!' Arden urged him.

He looked like a corpse.

Unless the letters were found, there was no way of fending off the shock. Odd twist, that Clarissa should have come here and done what Rollison had asked and forced him into this dilemma. He went quickly across the room, watched closely by the old man. He pushed the door to behind him and Arden called:

'Leave it open.'

He pulled the door open. Arden could see the desk and craned forward, peering into the study. Rollison pulled open the wide, shallow drawer in the middle. To see the back he had to go down on his knees. Arden couldn't see what he was doing now. The desk was a fine old piece of mahogany, beautifully finished inside. He ran his fingers along the smooth wood, seeking the spring.

He found it, pressed and heard a click. The false back of the drawer sprang open.

Arden cried: 'That's it. I heard it!'

The light was poor. Rollison saw some papers and pulled them out. There were two long, legal-looking documents, tied round with red tape. That was all; there were no letters. He could hear Arden's harsh breathing as he pulled off the tape and unfolded the documents. Both were wills. Neither contained any letters in their folds.

He drew back from beneath the desk.

Arden, standing in the doorway, croaked: 'They're gone,' and pitched forward on his face.

CHAPTER TWENTY

Challenge Accepted

'If he comes round again it will be a miracle,' the doctor said. 'You should have kept him in bed at all costs.' His voice was sharp and severe.

Rollison said: 'It would have helped if you'd stayed.'

'I have other patients. And I could not get a nurse quickly.'

'Let's stop arguing about it, shall we?' Rollison glanced down at the old man, whose face was blue from forehead to chin and who seemed hardly to be breathing. 'Do everything you can for him. If he can be pulled round again, he may be all right—I don't think there are any more shocks in store for him.'

The doctor said: 'This is a ridiculous business. First a woman who ought to know better excites him by quarrelling, then you— oh, never mind. Did you give him the good news?'

'Yes.'

'At least he had that,' said the doctor.

He turned away and Rollison went back into the study. He looked quickly through the two wills. One, dated several years ago, left a few minor bequests, a token legacy to Clarissa and the residue of the estate to Geoffrey Arden, described as 'my only son'. The other was dated eleven months ago—soon after the death of Geoffrey. Clarissa wasn't mentioned in it; there were no minor bequests; the estate was left to James Arden Mellor in its entirety. There were instructions about the efforts to be made to trace Jim if he had not been found at the time of Arden's death.

There was no doubt that old Arden hated Clarissa; yet he had allowed her to stay here.

Rollison went to the door and as he opened it the doctor called softly. 'Oh, Rollison.'

'Yes?'

'I'm sorry I spoke like that. The collapse must have been unavoidable. There was little I could have done, had I stayed—no one could have anticipated that he would get out of bed.'

'Of course not.'

'He'll probably want to see you if he comes round.'

'I'll be back as soon as I can.'

'Don't be too long, I beg you.'

The doctor went back and Rollison went quietly to the main landing and looked along the passage towards Clarissa's room. He went along to the room and pushed open the door but no one was there. The faint smell of perfume persisted. Rollison went downstairs and the butler came hurrying forward, to inquire:

'How is he, sir?'

'It's still touch and go. If Miss Clarissa returns I should like her to telephone me at once.'

'Very good, sir.'

Rollison nodded and the butler opened the door. As he did so, the rounded gleaming nose of Clarissa's car slid into sight. She stopped, glanced at the door, looked quickly away and sat quite still.

'Never mind that message,' Rollison said. 'And Miss Clarissa won't be coming in just yet.'

He went to the car and she drew in her breath and turned to face him. The window was down. He saw every line of her face: its soft loveliness; the strain at her eyes and her lips. Her vitality was at its lowest ebb.

'Where are the letters, Clarissa?'

'Destroyed,' she answered.

'Please don't lie.'

'That is the truth. How is he?'

'It's touch and go.'

'And I suppose you blame me for it?' She spoke without bitterness—in a tone of resignation; but the devil of suspicion tormented him. He could not be sure of her. This might be part of the deception which she had acted from the time they had first met.

Rollison said: 'Move over, will you?'

She obeyed and he got in, took the wheel and switched on the engine. He drove to Hyde Park, kept close to the near side and let the

251

car move slowly.

'It's no longer a question of blaming anyone. I asked you to look for papers—so if there's need to blame, blame me. Where are the letters?'

'I destroyed them.'

'Why did you do that?'

'I thought them best destroyed. No one will know what was in them now. If my uncle hadn't been an old fool he would have destroyed them a long time ago. They were blackmailing letters. He has been paying blackmail for several years.'

'When did you first know?'

'When I read the letters.'

'What did they say?'

'That is a family secret and I shall not tell you. If he wants to tell you, he can—but I doubt if he will. If he'd wanted to, he would have told you before.'

'If you didn't know what was in them, why did you take them?'

'I read the first letter and then had to read the others. They were just—blackmailing letters.'

'Written on pale blue paper, like his own?' asked Rollison softly and she turned her head and looked at him sharply. 'Like the note to Jim Mellor? And to Judith Lorne? I didn't tell you, did I, that your fingerprints were on those letters? I didn't tell the police, either, because I hoped there would be an explanation. I don't now.'

She said: 'Waleski asked me for some paper. I gave him several sheets.'

'So you took your note-paper to Paris! Try another version, Clarissa.'

She looked at him angrily.

'You are a hateful creature. I've told you the truth. I always take paper and envelopes in my writing-case when I travel. If you don't believe me, ask my maid.'

'There's too much hate in this business. There has been from the beginning—sheer, personal, malevolent hatred. Not crime for crime's sake, something even more corrupt and foul. Why was your uncle blackmailed, Clarissa? What crime had he committed in his youth?'

'Crime!' She laughed. 'No one is going to know what was in those letters. They're destroyed, gone for ever, and—'

'Who wrote them?'

'I could guess.'

'Why did you write them?' Rollison asked. The car was crawling now. He pulled into the side of the road, near the trees and the damp, bright grass. A dozen people passed and looked at them curiously but Rollison did not notice them. 'That's the answer, Clarissa, isn't it? You stole those letters and destroyed them because they were damning evidence against you. You blackmailed him, out of sheer malice: hatred. Why? What has he done to you?'

'Oh, you fool!' cried Clarissa. 'You fool!'

*   *   *

The late evening was cool and pleasant, the fresh green of trees and grass was soothing. Rollison drove three times round the Park. Not another word had been uttered since she had cried, 'You fool!' She looked straight in front of her, head held high, while he tried to sort out the confusion in his mind.

Was she still lying?

He wanted to believe her; that was why he was so determined to force her beyond endurance, to make her lose her temper and in so doing tell the truth. But after that one outburst she was composed with an unnatural calm that would not be easy to break.

If she had not written the letters, he believed he knew who had. He no longer thought that Arden might be the villain in some great conspiracy. Arden was the victim. Anxiety, fear, something near despair, had worsened his condition, had made the last years of his life an agony.

Had Clarissa been responsible?

If not, who hated him?

He said suddenly: 'I expect to meet your Mellor tonight,' and watched her closely.

She turned her head sharply. 'When? I don't believe you. How do you know him? How

254

could you arrange a meeting?'

'I don't know him. I've asked him to meet me.'

'Oh,' she said, and relaxed, gave a short, mirthless laugh. 'You're so omnipotent, aren't you? You've asked him to meet you and so of course he'll come cap in hand.'

'Gun in hand, more likely. But he'll come.'

'Why?'

'If I've done nothing else, I've switched some of the hatred towards me. It was turned on to my Mellor for a while—for far too long—but he's free of it now. Do you see what I mean, Clarissa?'

'How much do you know?'

'Nothing. But I think I know why you destroyed those letters.'

'Another bright idea?'

'I've told you one guess; there's another I'll keep to myself. I don't know which is right. If I meet Mellor, will you come with me?'

She said slowly: 'He'll never meet you.'

'That's begging the question. Will you come with me?'

'Yes,' she said.

'I think we'll go and wait at the flat,' said Rollison. 'I don't propose to let you out of my sight again.'

'I should be careful,' said Clarissa, tensely. 'A villainous shrew like me might cut your throat or stick a knife in your ribs. But if you're at your flat, the good Jolly will look after you, won't he? I'd forgotten how much you relied on Jolly. Why don't you take him with you to meet Mellor, instead of me?'

Rollison said: 'Because he doesn't hate Mellor.'

That pierced the brittle façade which she had built up about herself and they drove to Gresham Terrace in silence.

*   *   *

Grice had telephoned three times: would Rollison please ring him immediately he returned? Rollison went to the telephone and Jolly took Clarissa's hat and gloves, told her with his customary solemnity that she would find the mirror in the spare room best for making-up.

Grice was in his office, although it was after eight o'clock.

'Hallo, Bill,' Rollison said in a tone of near humility.

'What the devil's got into you now?' Grice barked: he was an angry Grice. 'What's this madness about challenging Mellor to meet you?'

'I thought you wanted to find him.'

'Don't play with words. I don't want you to commit suicide. I warned you he was gunning for you. You've gone completely crazy over this affair.'

'Oh, yes. As events have proved.'

256

'You're not to go to see Mellor. Understand?'

'Now, Bill, take it easy. You've had a man on my tail all the afternoon and I haven't shaken him off. If you want to put another squad on, do that. You've got the districts hotted up to look for Mellor—have 'em switched to me. But don't talk drivel, old chap. If I get a chance to see Mellor, I'm going to see him. It's the only hope I have of catching him. If you like to act the fool and follow me wherever I go, Mellor won't play and I can't win. If you think that will be a help, carry on.'

Grice said: 'I can't understand what's got into you.'

'You will,' said Rollison. 'Sorry I can't stop now.'

He put the receiver down and turned to see Clarissa coming from the hall. An appetising smell came from the kitchen and Jolly flitted across the room to the small dining-alcove where the table had been laid for one and was now laid for two.

'What wine will you drink, sir?' asked Jolly.

'Any choice, Clarissa?' asked Rollison.

'I'll leave it to you.'

'And I'll leave it to Jolly.'

'I hope you've given him instructions about your funeral,' Clarissa said.

There was iced melon; a meat pâté; roast chicken; trifle and Scotch woodcock; and first sherry, then champagne. The sight of the silver ice-bucket made Clarissa raise her eyebrows and she looked at Jolly as if understanding him at last. When he had gone she said:

'He has a grisly sense of humour.'

'He likes serving champagne at the end of the hunt.'

'You're sure it's over, aren't you?'

'Bar the last killing,' Rollison declared.

They were at the savoury when the telephone bell rang and Rollison betrayed his tension when he half-rose to answer it. Jolly came swiftly from the kitchen. Clarissa watched him intently. Jolly did not hurry, coughed as he put the receiver to his ear and announced solemnly:

'This is Mr Rollison's home.'

Rollison put a morsel of Scotch woodcock into his mouth. Clarissa fiddled with the long stem of the champagne glass.

Jolly said: 'Very well, Mr Ebbutt, I will tell him.' He put the receiver on the desk and turned; and tension was in him as well as the others. 'It is Mr Ebbutt, sir. He informs me that Mellor will meet you.'

CHAPTER TWENTY-ONE

Low Dive

'Mr Ar,' said Ebbutt into the telephone, 'if you take my tip, you won't go. You just won't go. It's arskin' for trouble. I wouldn't send a rozzer there to meet Mellor. It'll be your big mistake, Mr Ar, and the last one.'

'Where does he want me to go?' asked Rollison.

'Old Nob's. It's a low dive, Mr Ar—abaht the lowest in London. I wouldn't advise a friend o' mine to go there even if Mellor wasn't arahnd. You know the place—cor blimey, you know it, Mr Ar, if anyone does! It's where they 'ad that riot coupla' yers ago. The rozzers closed it up, remember; but it's opened again. New owner, same low dive. Two blokes neely got rubbed aht there. The dicks keep away from it mostly—never see one nowhere arahnd: they know it's not safe. You arsk Gricey, 'e'll tell yer.'

Rollison chuckled.

'He's told me. Old Nob's just the place, Bill. When am I to go there?'

'Arter ten o'clock tonight, but—'

'Any conditions?'

'No, Mr Ar. I got the squeak from a kid. Doan know 'ow Mellor got it to 'im. You know wot it's like: you never can trace back when anything comes along the vine. And becos there's no conditions I say it's dang'rous, Mr Ar. It's a trap. What could Mellor wanter see yer for if it wasn't to rub you aht?'

'No reason at all, Bill.'

'You don't get any better as you get older,' complained Ebbutt. 'Well, I s'pose I'll 'ave ter let yer go. But I'll 'ave that 'all packed—'

'Oh, no, you won't. Have two or three of your tougher boys there, if they volunteer to go—don't use any pressure on them, Bill. And you can spread your men round the hall outside—not too close. There are plenty of places they can go: all the pubs, Joey's—I needn't tell you. I'll call in at the Lion on my way; if the police are concentrating on the area, you can let me know there.'

'Okay,' said Ebbutt resignedly.

'You know the new owner at the place, don't you?'

'Yes. 'E don't want no trouble, neiver.'

'Tell him to have the stage trap-door clear,' Rollison said. 'That's important, Bill. I might lose if that's covered up.'

'I'll see to it, Mr Ar. But I tell you—'

'I'll come straight to you afterwards, Bill.'

'And 'oo's goin' ter carry you?' muttered Ebbutt. 'I wish you wouldn't go, Mr Ar.'

'So does Jolly,' said Rollison. 'I'll be seeing you.'

He put the receiver down and heard Clarissa

say: 'I've no influence at all with him, Jolly.'
She looked at Jolly. 'Well? You've fallen for it,
have you?'

'Yes.'

'Where are you to meet him, sir?'

'At Old Nob's.'

'Old Nob's!' exclaimed Clarissa. 'That's
where I met him before.'

She stood up and knocked a champagne
glass over. The champagne spread, still
bubbling, over the cloth, gradually soaked in
and became a dull wet patch.

'It is the most verminous, disreputable and
dangerous haunt in the East End of London,'
declared Jolly and drew in his breath. He
stood at attention and trembled slightly. 'I
think you must be out of your right mind to
contemplate going there to-night, Mr
Rollison, and I would be doing less than my
duty if I failed to say so.'

'You certainly would, Jolly. Care to change
your mind, Clarissa?'

'I'll come,' she said.

'Sir! You can't take Miss Arden, you really
can't!'

'We'll leave at nine o'clock and I'll make a
few calls first,' Rollison said. 'I shall go in
these clothes. I want the palm-pistol fully
charged both with ammonia pellets and
bullets—no shoulder holster, no ordinary
pistol. I'll take the sword-stick, too. Miss
Arden won't be armed.'

Jolly bowed, trembling.

'We'll have coffee now,' said Rollison. 'Then fetch the car from Pulham Gate. I want to be recognised by everyone.'

*   *   *

'I suppose if I ask you whether you really ought to go or whether you're planning it out of sheer stubbornness, you'll think I've lost my nerve or else have some sinister purpose,' Clarissa said. 'Can the police, the man Ebbutt and Jolly all be wrong?'

It was five minutes to nine.

'They're all quite right,' said Rollison.

'So you are crazy?'

'As crazy as Mellor. He may not turn up, of course. He probably won't. That's what the others fear. They think someone else will be waiting to cut me up. Old Nob's is notorious, if you need telling that. Probably Mellor's best move would be to stage another riot there with two or three toughs ordered to get me while the fun's going on. The police wouldn't be able to pin it on to anyone then. But my money's on his turning up.'

'Can you give me one good reason why he should?'

'Yes,' said Rollison. 'But you have to know your East End so as to understand it. You have to know your crooks, your gangs, the mentality of the leaders. You have to know

262

that the one besetting sin of them all is vanity. Mellor's gone all out to make himself a Big Boss. We've had few others in London but none has lasted so long. Every now and again someone who thinks he's cleverer than the rest has a cut at running the East End with all its profitable rackets. There are two ways to do it. One to work well in with everyone, be friendly, bribe your way. That takes a long time. The other way is to build yourself up a reputation for terrorising everyone else. Mellor's done that. He had two big plans; one has gone sour on him but the second might work because he still has his reputation. He hates my guts because I killed Waleski and saved "my" Mellor. That gives him one good reason for wanting me out of the way. There's a stranger reason still. Jolly should really tell you about it. I'm fairly well known in the East End. By a mixture of luck and judgment I've slapped down several of these would-be Big Boys. Now, if Mellor can slap me down— follow me?'

Clarissa actually laughed.

'That would set the seal to his fame?'

'He's crazy enough to think so, which makes us both crazy.' Rollison stood up.

'One more question,' said Clarissa. 'Why do you want me to come with you?'

'Why did you destroy those letters?'

'I think we'd better go.' Clarissa put out her cigarette as Jolly came in to say that it was four minutes past nine and that the car was waiting.

'Good,' said Rollison to Jolly. 'I'll be back late.'

'Yes, sir.'

Jolly did not say another word but, as the car moved off, Rollison saw him standing at the window of the sitting-room, looking out.

No police car followed them through the West or the East End; but Rollison knew that the police were on the look-out and reports of his progress were flashed back to the Yard and the Division by every policeman who saw the car.

*   *   *

By half-past nine the East End of London seethed with the news of the coming confrontation. Everyone in or on the fringe of the so-called underworld was agog with the story. Discussion in pubs and dives waxed hot, bookmakers did a brisk trade; and the betting was even, slightly in favour of the Toff, for purely sentimental reasons. A curious phenomenon became apparent as the hours passed. Men who hated the Toff as much as they feared him, and who hated and feared the police, hoped that he would win. Now and again a copper's nark slipped out of a pub and passed this information on to a detective; and it was sent back to Grice who was at

264

Divisional Headquarters. Excitement and disquiet bubbled everywhere but few knew where the meeting was to take place, although many guessed. No rumour that it was to be at Old Nob's reached Grice, who concentrated men near all known danger-spots and knew that nothing he could do would be in time to prevent trouble—only to clear up after it. When Mellor struck—and he would strike—it would be swift and merciless. Grice did not think Rollison had one chance in ten.

Probably the most worried man in the East End was Bill Ebbutt. He had given instructions to his countless cronies and had two or three reliable men at Old Nob's, where the dancing had started at half-past eight and by now was working itself up to its nightly, furious climax. He also had three men at the Lion, a dockside pub a few hundred yards away from the dance-hall.

One of them was Charlie who sported his canary polo sweater and a light brown cap and, for once, drank whisky: he needed something to keep his nerves steady. The Lion wasn't crowded: few pubs were that night. There were even fewer than usual at Old Nob's for many preferred to keep out of trouble, both for its own sake and because the lurking police would certainly raid as soon as the outbreak started.

No one doubted that the outbreak would come.

At twenty minutes to ten the door of the Lion swung open and a little man rushed into the smelly, smoky public bar.

'Charlie! Where's Charlie? Charlie, 'e's comin'! Car just turned the corner—'ear it?'

The gentle purr of Rollison's car sounded clearly through the hush which fell upon the room. Three men finished their beer and went out quickly, anxious to be clear of trouble; for the attack might come here. The car stopped and the twenty people in the room stood and watched the door; there was no pretence at normality. The barmaid, a middle-aged, tight-lipped woman, stood with her hand resting on her husband's big arm, also watching. No one drank; no one moved until Rollison stepped in and held the door open for Clarissa.

A gasp went up.

Rollison raised his silver-handled stick and said:

'Hallo, folks! Not drinking?'

No one answered but two or three people stirred. Eyes switched to Clarissa. Rollison laid his hand on her arm and led the way to the bar.

'Whisky, I think. Singles, Mrs Morley.'

The tight-lipped woman moved to the row of gleaming colourful bottles behind her and her hand shook as she measured out the whisky. Her husband put a jug of water and a bottle of soda-water on the bar. Charlie sidled up to Rollison and said:

266

'Bill says it's not too late to change yer mind, Mr Ar; an' no one will think any the worse of yer if you go back right now.'

'I've a call to make before I go home,' Rollison said. 'What'll you have, Charlie?'

'Double. The trap-door's fixed.'

'Good. Any police about?'

'Well, there is and there ain't,' said Charlie. 'They don't know where it's comin' off, so they've split up. 'Arf-a-dozen 'ere, 'arf-a-dozen there. You know 'ow it is.' He lowered his voice. 'You ain't takin' *er*, are you?'

'We're sight-seeing, Charlie.'

Charlie gulped. A low murmur of conversation buzzed, eyes turned from Rollison and Clarissa towards the clock which was five minutes fast. Clarissa seemed fascinated by the company, looked about her and said little to Rollison. She stood out among the cheaply-dressed women like a lily in a pond full of weeds. Her cheeks were slightly flushed and her eyes bright with excitement as much as nervousness.

The click ticked loudly.

Rollison finished his drink.

'I think we'll take a walk,' he said. 'Good night, all!' He took Clarissa's arm as the hands of the clock pointed to ten and Charlie slipped ahead and opened the door. He didn't speak again. They stepped out into the darkness of the street and the door closed behind them. At intervals gas-lamps broke the gloom; there

267

was hardly a sound.

They turned right.

'If we have to run for it, we shan't have time to start the car. They'll probably slash the tyres to ribbons if we take it too near Old Nob's, anyhow.'

'You ought to know.'

'I've a feeling that Mellor will be there,' Rollison said. But he said it largely to reassure her and with his free hand gripped the sword-stick lightly. The hand on Clarissa's arm was ready to move away in a flash at the first sign of trouble. The quietness of the night was sinister, secretive. Here and there were lighted windows and at most of the windows shadows of men and women. Sometimes they saw a couple standing against a door— watching. Everyone watched; no one spoke. Clarissa's footsteps rang out clearly as she kept pace with Rollison. A car passed the end of the road, headlights making a brilliant blaze.

'We turn left here,' said Rollison. 'Now listen carefully. When I shout "now!" scramble up on to the stage near the piano. Is that clear?'

'Yes.'

'Your life may depend on it.'

'And my reputation, Rolly, so that I can be trusted. Please believe in me.'

'You're here to prove I can,' Rollison said.

They turned the corner. Lights shone over the façade of a building which showed clearly

268

against the stars. That was Old Nob's and it was less than a hundred yards away. The sound of music came floating gaily through the air and Rollison felt Clarissa's arm go tense; but she didn't slacken her pace. Three cars stood outside the dance-hall with sidelights on. Half a dozen men stood about the entrance. As Rollison drew nearer, one of them slipped inside with the tidings. The lobby was poorly lit. Photographs of the band and the cabaret 'stars' who appeared nightly were stuck behind the glass fronts of small show-cases.

A strip of threadbare carpet led from the entrance to the pay-box and along a wide passage to the hall itself. A man with a broad, ugly face and oily dark hair, not unlike Waleski, sat in the pay-box, glowering as Rollison approached.

Rollison placed two half-crowns on the pay desk.

'You don't have to go in,' the man said.

'I do, Tick.'

'You're crazy.'

'Is Mellor here yet?'

The man named Tick did not answer but thrust two small pink tickets through the hatch. Rollison took them and gave them to Clarissa. She still wore the black-and-white check two-piece; her face was flushed and her eyes were even brighter than at the Lion. Music welled up—a rumba. The sliding noise of many feet on the polished floor came through the partly open door. A little man in a soiled, soup-spotted dinner-jacket stood by the door. He gulped as he took the tickets and opened the door for them to go through.

At the far end, on a low stage, a five-man band played frenziedly in the spotlight. On the floor, which was not overcrowded, a hundred couples danced with wild rhythmic abandon, laughing, grinning—or deadly earnest. A crowd gathered round the bar, in a corner near the door.

As if by clockwork, every head turned towards the door; even the band checked its swing and dancers missed their step. That was only for a second; they went on again swiftly; but there was less laughter, fewer people grinned or smiled and everyone watched Rollison and his partner, furtively or openly.

'Shall we dance?' asked Rollison.

Clarissa nodded.

Rollison hooked the sword-stick over his arm, led her to the floor and immediately whirled her into the thick of the dance. He knew in those few seconds that she was good; in spite of her tension, in spite of the watching eyes and the impending crisis, she danced easily and well; and gradually she began to warm up. They reached the stage and Rollison waved to the band-leader.

'Keep this one up, will you?'

The man didn't answer but the music went

on. Couples dropped out, too tired to go on, others came on the floor. Rollison seemed to give all his attention to the dancing, not to Clarissa; but he was watching as well as being watched. Not a face escaped his notice, hardly a movement. And Clarissa watched, too—looking for the sharp features and the beard of the man she knew as Mellor.

On and on; on and on—

Then a door by the side of the stage opened and Mellor came in with three men, one on either side and one behind him. He stood for a moment on the fringe of the dancefloor, then stepped on to it, towards Rollison and Clarissa.

CHAPTER TWENTY-TWO

The Big Boss

Tension sprang in the room—something which could be felt, which affected everyone from the band to the barkeeper, from the giddiest girl to the oldest man. More people left the floor, cautiously, anxious not to be noticed by Mellor. None came on; no more than fifty couples danced now. The band played with a new frenzy, in keeping with the moment of crisis.

Mellor reached Rollison and tapped his

shoulder.

Rollison said: 'Hallo,' and smiled and went on dancing; but Clarissa moved stiffly now and kept missing her step.

'My partner,' Mellor said.

'Oh—yes, of course. It must be an "excuse me", Clarissa.' Rollison surrendered her and Mellor took Clarissa in his arms. A sigh went up round the walls. Rollison glanced swiftly round, saw one of Ebbutt's men dancing with a blonde who had known younger days, went up to them. 'My dance?'

Ebbutt's man made a queer noise in his throat.

The blonde said: 'You've arst for it; you'll get it.'

'Scared?'

'You bet I'm scared!'

'Prefer not to dance with me?'

'I'll chance it,' she said. 'You *can* dance.'

She smiled tautly and swung her body to the rhythm. Rollison whisked her across the floor, slipped in between Mellor and Clarissa and the couple next to him. Clarissa was like a wooden block. Mellor held her tightly to him. More couples dropped out: the floor seemed empty now. Rollison scanned the doors and saw two men at each, powerful men, most of them obviously on guard. They were Mellor's men. So he had taken over Old Nob's. If the police came, if Ebbutt's men tried a raid, they would be unable to take anyone by surprise.

Outside there were runners, ready to rush in with the news of police approach. Mellor would not have taken the slightest chance tonight.

Mellor was grinning.

His dark, pointed beard made his face seem pale. His eyes glittered and he looked as if he had been drinking heavily. He was well-dressed—better than any man here, after Rollison. Except for the beard, there was nothing unusual about him.

He said clearly:

'You'll see who's the boss around here, sweetie.'

Clarissa didn't answer.

'Rollison thinks he's clever but he's going to find out his mistake.'

Rollison grinned across. 'That's what Waleski said.'

The smile faded. 'You don't have to remind me about Waleski. I was talking to Clarissa,' Mellor went on. 'Keep your mouth shut or I'll shut it for you.'

They danced on. The blonde brushed her hair back from her forehead; she was sweating.

'I can't stand this much longer,' she said. 'You were crazy to come here.'

'You won't have to stand it much longer.' They were near the band again and he winked at the band-leader and then stretched out his hand and touched Clarissa's arm.

'Enjoying yourself?'

She didn't answer.

'I told you—' began Mellor.

'Now, young Geoffrey, don't get cross,' said Rollison. He released the blonde, whispered: 'Go to the side,' and at the same moment Mellor dropped his arms from Clarissa. But he didn't take up a fighting attitude: he just stood there, dumbstruck, as if the 'Geoffrey' had drained away all his strength, as it had Clarissa's.

*　　　*　　　*

Geoffrey Arden.

*　　　*　　　*

Rollison shouted: 'Now!'

He grabbed Mellor round the waist and lifted him above his head as he snapped at Clarissa: 'On the stage—now!'

He reached the stage a yard behind her and stepped over the low front as the bandsmen stopped playing and scrambled away. Men came rushing towards them, knives flashed, women screamed, the lights went out.

Rollison yelled at Clarissa: 'The piano—hurry!'

She stumbled over a chair as torches shot out their bright beams. Mellor was kicking and struggling but still held above Rollison's head. A glow of light came from the front of the piano, from the ground. Clarissa was outlined against it.

A knife flashed across the room, struck the front of the piano and set the wires tinkling and trembling.

Ebbutt stood at the bottom of a flight of wooden steps leading from the stage trap-door to the cellar below. Rollison lowered Mellor and pitched him down.

A knife touched his shoulder, another the back of his hand.

Clarissa jumped down into the dimly lighted space below.

In the hall there was wild confusion, shouting, screaming, thudding footsteps. Men sprang on to the stage, cursing and roaring as Rollison jumped down. Ebbutt pulled the trap-door shut and rammed home the bolt. Feet and fists thudded on the door, the floor above their heads shook. A muffled roar rang out and a bullet smashed through the boards and sent a shower of cement chippings over Mellor, who lay helpless with Ebbutt's knee on his chest.

'All right, Bill—the passage,' Rollison said.

Rollison bent down and struck Mellor on the chin—a single blow enough to daze him. Ebbutt sprang towards a passage, where they were safe from shooting, pushing Clarissa in front of him. Rollison dragged Mellor. Several shots came, followed by more thumping.

Rollison brushed his hair back from his forehead.

'How long will it take the police to get here, Bill?'

'They won't be long,' said Ebbutt, and added fervently 'For once I'll be glad to see the baskets. I—*Listen!*'

High above the din came the shrill blast of a police whistle.

*   *   *

Ebbutt lifted Mellor up and policemen took him from the stage door while he was still dazed. Near the cellar passage, actually leading to a small props room but not to the street, Clarissa stood leaning against the wall. Rollison took her hands and said gently:

'It's all over, Clarissa.'

'I—I'm all right. So you knew—about Geoffrey?'

'Yes, I knew or guessed. Full story later; but there are things I must know now. Were those blackmailing letters from Geoffrey?'

'Yes.'

'Did they tell your uncle that Geoffrey led an East End gang and did Arden pay to stop a squeal to the police?'

'Yes.'

'Did you know Mellor was Geoffrey?'

'I—yes,' she said. 'Yes, that's why I hated him. It wasn't only the things he did to that

276

girl. I didn't know at first; it wasn't until I studied Geoffrey's photograph afterwards that—'

'*Rollison!*' Grice bellowed.

'Coming,' said the Toff.

He helped Clarissa up the wooden steps into the dance-hall, which was emptied of dancers now but was crowded at the doors by police, some in uniform, some in plain-clothes. They had made several arrests, not all of Mellor's men. Mellor, handcuffed, stood between two burly sergeants. He looked dazed and sick.

Jolly and Grice stood by the trap-door.

'Hallo, Jolly! I thought you didn't like trouble,' said Rollison. 'Feel like forgiving me?'

'We'll have the back-chat later,' said Grice but there was no harshness in his tone. 'You're the luckiest devil in England, Rolly. Are you hurt?'

'A scratch or two but nothing much. You were quick. Thanks.'

'We'd have been quicker if you'd told us where you were coming.'

'That would have kept Mellor away,' Rollison said. 'He made sure the rozzers weren't gathered here like bees round the old honey-pot.'

'All right—it's your night tonight,' Grice conceded with good grace. 'I'll give way to the Big Boss. How are you, Miss Arden?'

'Dazed,' said Clarissa. 'Dazed and

277

marvelling. I know how people do the impossible now.' She laughed, weakly. 'It was impossible, wasn't it? I—I think I'd like a drink, Rolly. I must have—'

Jolly bent down and opened an attaché-case. 'Whisky, gin or brandy, Miss?' he asked.

*   *   *

Clarissa sat in Sir Frederick Arden's leather armchair, at his desk; Rollison in the smaller chair; Grice on a corner of the desk. The door leading to the bedroom was closed. In there the doctor was still with Arden, who had not yet come round; he would probably recover from this seizure but his days were running out fast. A nurse was with them. At a small table a detective-sergeant sat with pencil and notebook, working hard. It was nearly one o'clock but none of them seemed tired.

'It's a long, grim story, Bill, and the primary motive was hatred,' Rollison said quietly. 'Clarissa will put me right on details where she can. I know a little and guess a great deal but I don't think there'll be much wrong with the general outline. The hating began some years ago, when Geoffrey Arden learned to hate his father. I don't know why, but—'

Clarissa said: 'Geoffrey was always a misfit. I once told you that his father tried to make him a spineless fool but there was strength and a streak of cruelty in him—there always

278

had been. The Commando training brought it out. His father tried to knock it out of him at first, then to protect him against it—and didn't succeed. I know the old man doted on him; I was always afraid that Geoffrey hated his father.'

Rollison said: 'The cruelty was there all right. And it's obvious now that when Geoffrey started this so-called slumming he actually worked with the Dimond Gang and, with his strong personality, took it over.

'He wanted to hurt his father, to wound him savagely.

'He started by sending anonymous blackmailing letters, saying he was the head of the gang, making his father pay substantial sums so as to keep the secret. A warped mind; but the trick worked well. It reached a stage when Arden discovered who was behind the blackmail. He paid for the silence but altered his will, switching over to his illegitimate son. Not a surprising thing in the circumstances. There must have been a hell of a quarrel and Geoffrey pretended to be burned to death. We'll probably never know who really died.

'Geoffrey traced Mellor, bought a big interest in Mellor's firm, through Flash Dimond's brother, and so had Mellor where he wanted him—always at hand. He arranged that Mellor should spend some time in the East End, mixing with Galloway and other members of the gang; and he himself adopted

279

the name of Mellor. Then he let news trickle through to his father: Mellor, the other son, was as bad as the first. See the fiendish cruelty of it? But Arden wasn't convinced, couldn't believe it would happen twice, suspected what might be the truth—remember Geoffrey's body had been unrecognisable, he'd been identified by pieces of clothing, a ring on his finger and a watch—and he asked me to trace Mellor.

'Geoffrey was still hard at work.

'He schemed to get one of the gang on the staff here, another at Arden Lodge. He knew his father was afraid of his weak heart, worked on that not by poisoning him but, through the treacherous servants, diluting his medicine. Crafty and clever. It was all part of the general plan to hurt and wound his father.'

Grice said: 'Yes, I've come across that kind of thing.'

'The final crushing stroke was to have Mellor accused of a murder he himself had committed and to have Mellor hanged. And there was cunning behind that, Bill. With Mellor dead, any second will would be discounted and as next-of-kin Geoffrey would inherit. He would have been able to prove his identity; you'll find he'd arranged that. Men have popped up again after being pronounced dead often enough before. The plan went wrong when my Mellor escaped from the police. On the one hand, Geoffrey was gloating over the torment that the police hunt for Mellor gave his father, he told Arden of Mellor's identity by telephoning him. On the other hand, he was worried because Mellor was eluding the police. Another factor he hadn't reckoned on intruded when I began to work for Arden. No one with Geoffrey's reputation in the East End could fail to know—sorry, Clarissa!—about the Toff. Members of the gang would warn him and get him on edge. He saw the possibility that Mellor mightn't be convicted. All right then: get rid of him, quickly.'

'Why didn't he kill him?' asked Grice.

'A straightforward murder wouldn't have suited his purpose; there was a risk of the murderer being traced. So he tried to drive Mellor to suicide, planned to leave that "confession" note behind. He used Waleski for the job and tried to involve Clarissa. A silly thing but he wouldn't see it that way. Clarissa had seen him, could identify him, so she had to die sooner or later. But why not add to the total of his father's mental torment? Give me grounds for thinking Clarissa was also involved—as she was, unwittingly—and make a thorough job of it; and then have Clarissa murdered? More agony—while he himself would be sitting pretty?

'Only it didn't work out like that.

'When it was known that Jim Mellor was safe and Clarissa's evidence would prove he

281

wasn't the gangster, Geoffrey had only one thing to fall back on: his reputation in the East End. He saw that he could establish an impregnable position if he could get rid of me. I gave him the chance, convinced that he wouldn't be able to resist it. I had two reasons for wanting to catch him, Bill. The ordinary reason, that I don't like men of Geoffrey's corruptness holding sway in the East End; another that I may tell you about one day.'

'Tell him now,' urged Clarissa, and went on without giving Rollison a chance to speak. 'He thought I was involved, Mr Grice. He wanted to make me break down and confess or give myself away when I met Geoffrey again.'

Grice said: 'Hrrrumph!'

Rollison smiled: 'Thanks, Clarissa! Bill owes you apologies, too. I don't think there's much else, Bill. If Arden recovers enough, he'll be able to confirm most of it, I think. You'll get one of the gang to squeal too, although you won't get much out of Geoffrey.'

'We'll get enough to have him hanged,' Grice said. 'Well, you'll have to explain again in court—and so will Snub, about the cottage.'

'Gladly,' Rollison assured him.

Grice stood up from the desk and, as he did so, the door opened. The doctor came in, looking weary but smiling and rubbing his hands together.

'Believe it or not, he's conscious—and asking for you, Mr Rollison.'

*   *   *

Rollison said to the old man: 'Yes, it's all known, all over. Tomorrow I'll bring the boy Mellor to see you.'

*   *   *

Rollison opened the door of his flat and Clarissa stood there, a vision in dark green with a wide-brimmed hat which set off her beauty to perfection. He took her hands and drew her into the hall.

'Where's Jolly?' she asked.

'Out.'

'Discreet Jolly,' murmured Clarissa. 'I was wrong about him. You would wither up without your Jolly.'

'Thanks!'

She laughed as they went into the living-room, stepped across to the trophy wall and took a sheet of pale blue notepaper and a drawing-pin from her bag. She fastened the paper on to the noose of the rope and stood back to admire the effect.

'Do you like it?'

'I'll treasure it.'

'I hope you will.'

'Rely on it. Clarissa, why didn't you tell me about the letters; about Geoffrey?'

'Would you have believed in me then? I

don't think so. There was only one way to convince you.' She looked into his eyes, her own smiling but touched with hurt; or with longing. 'Rolly, I've tried to think clearly during the past three days, since it ended. I've some things straight. I want, I need, a quieter life—for a while. You thrive on excitement, sensation; it's the basis of your life.'

'Proposal withdrawn?' asked Rollison gently.

'Postponed. Until, if ever, it comes from you to me.'

ABERDEEN
CITY
LIBRARIES